YOU, ME &

A Celebration of Writing in First and Second Person

Edited by S Philip

Stories Written by

Hettie Ashwin	E A M Harris
Kim Bannerman	Dora L Harthen
Cath Barton	Kati N Hendry
Sharon Birch	Debz Hobbs-Wyatt
Miki Byrne	Julia Hones
Walter Campbell	Amy Hulsey
Charlotte Comley	Alexis A Hunter
Annemaria Cooper	Michelle Ann King
Meriah L Crawford	Deborah Klée
Stefanie Dao	Tanya Jacob Knox
Simone Davy	Meg Laverick
Laura Dunkeyson	Diane Lefer
Sarah Evans	Diandra Linnemann
Anne Fox	Nina Milton
Robert Lee Frazier	Monika Pant
Martin Gamble	Emma Phillips
Susan F Giles	Barry Pomeroy
Heidi Gilhooly	Zena Shapter
Anne Goodwin	Jay R Thurston
Margaret Gracie	Abigail Wyatt
Cathryn Grant	Zarina Zabrisky

Published By
Chuffed Buff Books Ltd

Published by Chuffed Buff Books Ltd.
London, United Kingdom
www.chuffedbuffbooks.com

ISBN 978-1-908858-02-3

You, me & a Bit of We
A Celebration of Writing in First and Second Person
Copyright © Chuffed Buff Books, 2013

Typeset in Minion

First published in United Kingdom, 2013
Printed by Lightning Source

YOU, ME & A BIT OF WE

A Celebration of Writing in First and Second Person

WWW.CHUFFEDBUFFBOOKS.COM

YOU, ME & A BIT OF WE

This collection is a showcase of 42 stories written in either second, first or first person plural point-of-view. Through flash fiction and short stories, readers are invited to discover their favourite seat in a story. Is it front row centre, in the midst of a crowd, or from a more personal vantage point? Where second person thrusts the reader into an active role, first person offers experience through the eyes of an individual or group. Although the use of first person is common, second and first person plural perspectives are relatively rare.

Written by an international cast of authors, *You, Me & a Bit of We* includes a broad range of themes. There are tales of transition, conviction, lost love, grief, conflict, domestic strife, tragedy, second chances, and stories about letting go and moving on. There are worlds where it is rare to be sighted, skin tells a story, past lives haunt, deadly viruses and parasites threaten humanity, and death is personified.

From the poignant to the fantastical, dark, witty and uplifting, each story in this anthology is original, thought provoking, and reflective of the versatility of perspective as a literary device.

&

Contents

1. Your final Engagement *Martin Gamble* 1
2. Death's Mistake *Meg Laverick* 4
3. Sidewalk Shouting *Walter Campbell* 9
4. The Bedroom Mirror *Anne Fox* 14
5. Home Strange Home *Diandra Linnemann* 16
6. The Bridge over the River Illias *Robert Lee Frazier* 18
7. Marathon to Perfection *Margaret Gracie* 20
8. Lily *Hettie Ashwin* 22
9. At The Edge of the Mattress *Annemaria Cooper* 25
10. That Loving Feeling *Sharon Birch* 27
11. To Light a Candle *Heidi Gilhooly* 29
12. Odds *Sarah Evans* 34
13. Gonnagetya *Meriah L Crawford* 41
14. Toxoplasme *Stefanie Dao* 46
15. Blood Song *Alexis A Hunter* 52
16. You Weren't Heavy *Laura Dunkeyson* 53
17. Last Funeral But Two *E A M Harris* 60
18. The End of the Line *Cathryn Grant* 67
19. The Illuminated Back *Nina Milton* 70
20. A World of Difference *Deborah Klée* 78
21. Cockle Shells *Simone Davy* 86
22. When the Wind Changes *Debz Hobbs-Wyatt* 91
23. Got You *Amy Hulsey* 97
24. Birdfeed *Emma Phillips* 104
25. The Second Coming *Cath Barton* 109
26. A Galilean Quartet *Abigail Wyatt* 111
27. Crisis of Personality *Miki Byrne* 114
28. Free to Loving Home (Donation Required) *Michelle Ann King* .. 116
29. The Crowning *Jay R Thurston* 118
30. I Have God to Thank for Everything *Barry Pomeroy* 123
31. A Hospital in Latin America *Julia Hones* 129
32. True Love *Diane Lefer* 135
33. Your Famous Pink Raincoat *Susan F Giles* 138

34.   DON'T BREAK MY HEART   *Charlotte Comley* 145

35.   OUR RELATIONSHIP WITH THIEVES   *Kati N Hendry* 150

36.   LOST TO THE RISING TIDE   *Kim Bannerman* 155

37.   AVA, LEIGH, SARAH, MINNIE, ANNIE, AND ME   *Zarina Zabrisky*... 157

38.   THE COLOURS OF HER SOUL   *Monika Pant*................................. 162

39.   PONY HARRIS   *Tanya Jacob Knox* 167

40.   ISLAND ROCKS   *Dora L Harthen* 169

41.   OUR SOMETHING SAID   *Zena Shapter* 172

42.   A HOUSE FOR THE WAZUNGU   *Anne Goodwin* 180

You, Me & a Bit of We

A Celebration of Writing in First and Second Person

Your Final Engagement
Martin Gamble

You sit alone in your armchair, waiting. I'm hiding in the darkest corner of the room as you rest in silence, unaware that I'm staring at you. From the viewpoint of anyone passing by it would appear as though you're quite content. But from my all seeing eyes, I know you're riddled with uncomfortable thoughts, and your mind is unable to find the off switch you desperately seek.

The years have trickled through your fingers and you wonder how on earth you became so terribly old. Even to the newly retired generation you're classed as very old. Sometimes you struggle to remember exactly how old you are. You've lived alone for the past few years and your family visits you once a week. Soon, they will come again. To check you're okay. To check you're still alive. You have a helper who comes every Monday at noon, but it's Thursday now and despite the hunger pangs you know your bad leg and stiff back aren't yet ready to carry your fragile body to the kitchen.

A power cut two hours ago sent your house into darkness whilst you were watching TV. You sit awake in your front room with only the distant glow of an emergency solar streetlight. It acts as a simple compass to denote the direction of the window. You can't use your stair lift so it's impossible to get to your bedroom, or climb into bed, during the blackout. You dread waking up in the night when your arthritic joints begin to scream for relief, and in some ways you're thankful for an evening without your endless grooming rituals. In a dire emergency, you know you can always call on the couple next door for help.

You've nothing else to do but sit and wait until the lamp or the TV flashes back into action. As you sit patiently in your armchair, with time hopelessly passing by, your imagination is your only source of entertainment. You begin to patch together your most memorable days during each year of your life. This proves to be both distracting and relaxing. You hit a snag when you remember the most regretful time of your life, but then you quickly refocus your attention on the good old days, flipping through your scrapbook of memories, until the smile on your face reappears.

You stop short when you notice my presence in the room. Your eyes remain closed. You've already guessed the identity of my unique existence looming toward you from the shadows.

'It's you, isn't it?' You utter your first words in three days.

'Yes,' I answer in a flat and emotionless voice. 'This is the end.'

'I've been wondering when you'd come.' Your breathing slows and you sink further into your armchair. 'I'm ready. I am. I really am.'

'You are not ready.'

'What do you mean I'm not ready?'

At first I'm silent and take no action. Then I force the pages of your memory scrapbook to start turning once again, but now it only contains my biased account of your lifelong regrets and sorrows. I hit you with a barrage of grim moments from your life. You understand perfectly because you're fluent in your own melancholy.

'That's why.'

You start to breathe faster and it's clear that what I've shown you has evoked an emotional response. Anxiety begins to take hold and your face tightens, pumped with blood and pressure. A cyclone in your mind catches the pages of the scrapbook, turning them over, wildly out of control.

'But I thought this was the end for me. You said my time ends here!'

'This is the end and your path ends here, although your time is not yet up.'

You begin to notice an eerie ticking sound that's unfamiliar to you. *Tock, tick, tock tick.* It sounds backwards, but you're confused as to whether it's just your clouded interpretation. It speeds up and becomes a banging that reverberates through your skull. You feel like you're upside down and your feet are bent backwards around your head. You become dizzy like in the last few moments of consciousness before an anaesthetic takes hold.

I scoop up your dying existence in my makeshift hands, but instead of sending you upwards or downwards, I catapult you backwards, sending you hurtling through the air and as far away from me as possible. You travel at incredible speed, developing a warm inner-glow that comforts your bewilderment and begins to peel away your old and dying outer layers.

You experience so many feelings, thoughts and sensations that your mind struggles under the strain and starts to collapse. You can't hold on any longer and you let go, sending your consciousness into darkness and your senses into nothingness.

Your mind reawakens and tunes in to the sound of my voice, telling a story about a possible future you. Yet, you are in the here and now, and you're not old anymore. I'm guessing you feel normal, or possibly even great. Understandably, there's some confusion as to what it is I've done to you, or what it is I've done *for* you.

My story comes to an end and you continue on your beautiful path. We will meet again, many years from now. I will tell a story, perhaps the same story, or maybe a different one. Either way I expect you will welcome me with open arms, a glad heart and—most importantly— without regret.

DEATH'S MISTAKE
Meg Laverick

You don't really know when you came into being. You leave that work for philosophers and fanatics to fight over. What you do know is that you're there when he opens up his eyes for the first time and looks around at this funny life he's been given.

What you do know is that you'll be the last thing he'll see when his funny life has come to a close and it's time for you to guide him away.

His mother smiles down at him, ignoring the mess of birth as she holds him closely. You know that she has something similar to you looking over her shoulder at all times, watching. You can't see it, but every living thing has one. Life's constant companion. She smiles as she gives him his name. Jim. The one you're destined to follow as long as he shall live. Even as he looks around his new world, you're there, ready to take him away. But you don't, not yet.

In the manner of all children, Jim is blissfully unaware of your existence. He's like any normal child: too inquisitive for his own good and not forward-thinking enough to recognise consequences.

He first becomes dimly aware of you when he unthinkingly takes his goldfish out of the bowl, fascinated to see it flap as it gasps for air. You watch too. You've never seen something die before. You've never seen the way it struggles for life. Even one second longer in this world is a victory. You've never seen the way living things finally accept their death and slip gracefully into that good night, acquiescing to their fate after a long struggle. There's a beauty in that. You're glad you're part of that dance.

Jim yells at the goldfish to wake up again. His yelling attracts his mother who tuts at him and explains the order of the world, how eventually everyone is taken away.

He turns and you feel his cold, fearful gaze on you. It's the first time he's been aware of your ever-watchful gaze and he's frightened. He doesn't want to be taken away from this life. Not yet. He's barely begun living. He doesn't want to struggle like the goldfish.

You reach out to touch him, trying to reassure him that it isn't his time. He's still of the living world and doesn't need to fear the unknown. In your touch you try to convey that even when he does depart you'll be there, someone who watched and celebrated every living moment, who will guide him through to a different kind of living. You don't know what you'll guide him towards, but you know he'll have a friend with him.

He shivers and turns away from you, seeking comfort in his mother's warm, living arms. He doesn't want your friendship.

You try not to feel hurt at his rejection. He doesn't understand that one day, just like the goldfish, he'll welcome you as a reward after his struggle. But not yet.

He forgets you most of the time, carrying on with the business of living. Every so often something will happen that makes him glance your way before he scowls and turns his back on you.

It's not until he's a teenager that he ever really gives you serious thought, dramatising your work in his head and recognising the beautiful dance you first witnessed when performed by a lowly goldfish.

He reads about you and actively wonders what it'd be like to take your hand and escape. But then the brilliance of life distracts him and he's once again lost to you. You secretly breathe a sigh of relief whenever this happens. You don't want to take away the vibrancy and colour of Jim's life. Not yet.

And he doesn't want to leave either. Not really. Though he gives it lip service, he's not ready to take your hand just yet. When he climbs into a car with one of his friends who's had a bit too much alcohol, he fears for his life. He doesn't want to die. He wants to keep living in the world, to struggle against the all-consuming unknown you will one day lead him toward.

You stand guard over him as he lies unconscious on the road, his legs at awkward, unnatural angles. You see his friend's crumpled form, thrown a few metres away from where you stand—he has lost the fight. You cannot see it but you can feel that his Death has taken him into the great unknown.

Jim lies very still. You can still see his chest rise and fall and you're not worried. You know that it's not his time; it's not your time. Not yet.

When Jim grows up and moves away to university, you follow him. You've watched him grow from a squalling, selfish child to a reckless, self-absorbed teenager and finally into the handsome, confident young man that you happily claim as yours. You know that when the day comes for him to be taken away it won't be simply a job anymore. You will wrap your arms around him and comfort him, telling him that he's done well. A life lived beautifully.

You watch as he meets a girl at a party, red, plastic beer cup in hand. He toasts her across the room and she smiles. You watch helplessly as he's drawn in by her charm. There is a wrongness about this encounter. You try to stop him, placing a hand on his shoulder. There's something telling you to get away, to forget this ever happened.

You can only watch as they smile and begin talking.

Despite your misgivings, you have to admit the beauty of it. The way Jim expands, lighting up the whole room whenever she is there. The way their sweet kisses highlight the joy of life, and the way they hold each other securely in bed, speaks of their desire to stay here, in this moment, in this life forever.

But you can also see the costs. The way Jim will give up everything in order to achieve those moments of beautiful living. The way he'll give it up at the expense of everything else. While once Jim would constantly light up the room with his exuberance and joy for life, now he saves it all for her.

You can't do anything. You try, pointing out the beauty of the small things: the warmth of the sun hitting his face, the way people can talk to each other without ever having to speak a word, the way the softness of cotton feels on his skin. You try to show him the joy of life he's lost; you try to bring him back to the world she doesn't exist in.

But he ignores you. He's in his early twenties and he believes he's invincible. After obsessing over you in his teenage years, he's now come to terms with your constant presence. He just doesn't look. It's a compromise that allows him to live without fear.

You can feel it. You can feel his time coming to a close. The siren call of your duty is faintly on the horizon and you'd do anything to avoid it. You're not ready to say goodbye to him. You're not ready to lead him through that veil. Not yet. Not quite yet.

The day the siren reaches you, loud and clear, is a day like any other. Jim is blissfully unaware while you spiral down into despair. You don't want this. Not yet. It can't be his time yet.

He picks up his wallet and shoves it in his pocket before heading out. He's going to her place. He likes to do this every other morning, just to check in, to get that buzz of life-giving love. He's suggested that they move in together several times but she's resisted, saying that she needs space and that he needs to be understanding.

He's left a bit later than usual, having slept in. You spent your time watching over him while he slept, memorising every detail and taking joy in every movement of his chest. It's not his time. He's still too alive. Too alive for you. You're not needed yet.

He rounds the corner to her apartment building. You see a smile light his face as he recognises her shining blonde hair at the doorway. He's about to call out to her when she's joined by someone he doesn't recognise. The smile turns to horror as she reaches up to caress his cheek before kissing him sweetly and passionately—the same way she kissed Jim only a few nights ago. He stands rooted to the spot as he watches.

The sirens have become a screaming in your ears. It's almost time. Almost time for you to do the terrible duty you were put on this earth to do. And you're not ready.

After staring for long enough to bring tears to his eyes, blurring his vision, he turns to stumble away. He needs to escape; he can't be in this place anymore. He can't watch them together. He walks behind a parked van and steps out on to the street.

He doesn't have a chance to see the truck and the truck certainly doesn't have a chance to see him. As he dashes the tears from his eyes he has less than a second to grasp the enormity of his mistake. A second in which he thinks about her.

The sirens cease.

You look down at his broken body, made unrecognisable by the impact. You're not ready for this. You're not ready to see your Jim left like this. You're not ready to take him away from the beauty of life. It isn't his time to stop fighting. It can't be. Because it isn't your time to embrace him. Not yet. Not yet.

So you hide. You shirk your duty hoping that your refusal to take him into death will mean that he has the chance to live on. You hope that by refusing to hold his hand you will force him to stay in that broken body, to keep breathing.

But you are wrong. From your hiding spot you see him leaving the life you have so cherished. You see him abandon the body that has sheltered him and given him life. But, bereft of his guide, he is lost and frightened. He should have your hand to take; he should have your arms to guide him. But you are not there. He looks around bewildered for a second before the ether takes him away.

You stare after him, feeling the cold and empty feeling of regret. What have you done? You tried to save him, but now he is lost to you forever. You didn't guide him to that other place and he couldn't get there himself. He is lost and you were the one to lose him.

You are bereaved because you cannot embrace him. You cannot thank him for everything, for the life he has led and for the joy he has given you. You can do none of that. You missed your chance. You can only stare after him and feel the thread of life escaping you. The coldness wraps around you, reminding you that without him that is all you are. There is no one to take you out of this nightmare and into the beyond. There is no vibrant spark of life to rejoice in. Not anymore.

There is only you.

SIDEWALK SHOUTING
Walter Campbell

W HEN you first wake up you think of blueberry pancakes, French vanilla coffee and how badly you have to pee. You think of the dream you had about your kindergarten teacher and your neighbour's Pomeranian getting into an argument in front of the farmers' market where you buy honey and apples but talk to no one because you hate the people at farmers' markets. The customers, not the farmers. You think of when your milk will go bad and how much time you have to shower. You think of how dirty your carpet is and if you'll have time to vacuum. You even think of what part of your body itches most.

But you never think of God.

Ed, on the other hand, does.

This is not to suggest that Ed doesn't eat pancakes, drink coffee, urinate, dream, buy milk, shower, clean his apartment, or even itch in indecent places. It is just that before and during all those things he thinks about God, and this is what fascinates you about Ed. His cat—a short, chubby grey cat with long hair that gathers under his bed in tennis-ball-sized patches—is very similar to your short, chubby grey cat. His cat, like yours, doesn't much care for religion. They prefer canned food and the sounds of mice in the walls. Since Ed's cat was listening to the mice all night, he now has canned food on his mind and Ed obliges, much like you oblige your own cat. However, instead of thinking, *my fat cat needs some food so he has the energy to rip up my furniture and get hair all over my apartment*, Ed thinks the much more noble, *I feed this cat because he is one of God's glorious creations*. Otherwise, your relationships with your respective cats could not have been more similar.

Halfway through his second pancake Ed starts running through verses he might quote that day—much like you run through CNN articles—until he settles on a solid ten. Next, as you're checking traffic, programming your GPS, and browsing through email, Ed's picking out his preaching locations. He'll start near a college (drinking in excess and fornicating out of wedlock), then he'll move downtown (adulterous,

.ng businessmen). He'll fill the afternoon with a moderately dangerous neighbourhood (drug dealers and their victims, prostitutes and their clients), and finally he'll end the evening in his own upscale neighbourhood (love thy neighbour). He tests his bullhorn twice while you fuss with your hair. He makes sure his crucifix t-shirt isn't wrinkled and doesn't hang too far over his jeans, secures his mini Bible in his right pocket, checks his backpack for ten extra Bibles, and fills a huge water bottle. You put a little make up on, make sure you have all your textbooks, and pack a quick lunch.

Thirty minutes later, Ed is standing near a dormitory bullhorning the gospel as little droplets of sweat begin—the products of wearing jeans during the humidity of a Mid-Atlantic summer. Meanwhile you work in the building across the street, running through your class notes for the day. You head outside for a coffee, not sweating at all since your work environment is air-conditioned.

First you hear him and it sends an odd warmth through you that you can't quite classify, and this annoys you. Ed is bellowing *thees* and *haths* above all the other noises of the city, like a howler monkey screaming over an army of jungle birds. You look, trying to find the source of his voice and, when you finally see him, are shocked to see a handsome young man spouting off like a homeless guy on a subway platform.

Today, Ed notices you—in your slightly less than conservative dress—with a grimace of disgust. It's that forceful look that sets you off on a direct path towards him. You've thought of approaching him before but today you actually do it. As you get closer, as he sees you, a quick shiver runs through him.

'Hi, there! What do you think of Buddhism?' you ask. For you, this is a perfectly valid opening. Ed lowers his bullhorn and tells you flatly, almost timidly, that he doesn't like it.

'Great! Let's go get some coffee,' you suggest, rejoicing in how shocked he is by this. 'To further discuss religion, and because I need coffee before my first class.' You place a hand on his shoulder. He shudders and you feel the need to explain further. 'I'm a professor of religion here. I'd love to discuss religion with you.'

Ed is just as apprehensive as you are eager. He can't, he simply can't. He must stay here, firmly at his post, doing God's work as he has done so diligently every day for the past four years. Besides, coffee with a woman he just met wouldn't be appropriate. Or at least that's what you think must be running through his sweating head.

'Yes, I think that would be a good idea,' Ed says, just as shocked at the words leaving his mouth as you are. You laugh because of the formal way he speaks and because you think it will lighten his mood a little, and the two of you walk to a small, empty place a few blocks away. You order an iced-coffee, like someone should on such a hot day, and Ed orders a hot coffee, adds no milk, and soon you notice him sweating into his drink, awkwardly trying to wipe it away with the little napkins they have near the sugar.

'How long have you been preaching to passers-by?'

'Four years,' he says through a drop of falling sweat.

'Four years is a long time.'

'Yes, but not long enough. I couldn't start until my parents passed away. They left me an inheritance and I was able to quit my job and devote my time to the cause.' You nod quickly, but ignore what he's said. You really don't want to know any of his motivations. You feel sick when other professors in your field bring up their personal reasons for studying religion. You don't want to hear it, not one bit. For you, it's like listening to a couple baby talk to each other. Hearing that and knowing someone's religious background both feel like an invasion of privacy.

But Ed doesn't want to tell you any more about his parents. He wants to tell you about a guy named Jesus, but he doesn't want to tell you why he cares about a guy named Jesus. And that's so very nice, so very refreshing.

'Have you ever converted anyone?' you can't help but ask.

'Of course, on many occasions,' he lies.

Ed looks as though he wants to run, but then a second later he appears happy where he is. He's fighting himself like a masochistic military in which the army attacks the navy. You do him the favour of not looking him in the eye too often as you talk about religion, and even though he's fighting himself, he seems to enjoy it overall. Jesus this, Buddha that, Siddhartha, Mary, Ten Commandments, Eightfold Path, and Jesus; or something like that.

A half hour later, you tell him you have a class but would like to continue the conversation over dinner. He hesitates at first as if coffee with a female professor is fine in God's eyes, but dinner, simply, is not.

'I'd love to. How about the Indian place down the street?' Ed blurts and, once again, you are both surprised by his response.

You set a time and go your separate ways. You teach college students about enlightenment and while you lecture on the difficulty of having an empty mind, Ed sweats it out near businessmen and lawyers who throw him change, mistakenly thinking he's homeless.

Once he's back near campus—doing a little extra preaching to make up for what he'd missed earlier—Ed fights the urge to go home, shower, change clothes, and put on more deodorant. He can't remember the last time he felt the need to look or smell nice, and it worries him.

In the end he doesn't shower and change but you do, and he notices. Ed wants to think himself a sinner for noticing, but you smile in a way that melts the arctic and his worry fades without struggle.

'How was your day?' you ask.

'It was great,' he lies and reaches awkwardly for a samosa

You and Ed continue talking about God. A few times, when you move your legs, you notice that he reddens, but you smile and his normal colour returns. After chicken tikka masala, you invite him back to your place to look at some texts you use in class, and he accepts.

Once there, Ed tells himself to leave; he's an object of your lust or he's just a weird fish in your academic tank.

But he stays and after you show him a few books that discuss the parallels between Christianity and Buddhism, and after he lovingly pets your cat, telling you that she looks just like his cat, you lean in and kiss him. And when you kiss him he doesn't put an end to it because his mind has quieted completely. Free of all thoughts. So free that when you do more than kiss him, he doesn't stop it.

Ed wakes up late, hours later than he usually does, but he doesn't rush from bed. He looks at you smiling in your sleep, dreaming of old teachers and neighbours' Pomeranians, and his urgency fades like summer rain.

Ed gets dressed and says goodbye without waking you.

Almost instinctively he walks to the place where you had coffee yesterday. He orders an iced-coffee like you would. He doesn't sweat into it, but at one point, out of habit, reaches up to his forehead to wipe away sweat and when he finds none, his formerly contained self-hatred swells like a recent bruise collecting blood. Ed is suddenly disgusted with his iced-coffee. He throws it violently in the trash and half of it spills on the floor. Meanwhile you stir in your sleep, having moved on to a dream about two large dogs barking at each other.

A barista with tattoos and a nose ring yells at Ed to clean up his mess.

'I *am* cleaning up my mess!' Ed yells back, running out of the coffee shop. He continues three blocks west at full speed, heading to the spot on campus where he last neglected his duties. He is late so he rushes, sprinting as you sleep.

But when he gets to the block, he feels his energy evaporate like he's just lost all his blood sugar. At the end of the street, right where his post is, there's a man with a bullhorn.

'Believe in God, accept Jesus as your own personal saviour or burn in Hell!' The man yells over and over.

Ed can't move from where he stands, he can't stop staring, and he can't say a thing. The man notices Ed and turns to him. He glares in complete silence for almost a minute, and then repeats his mantra.

All the while he looks straight into Ed's eyes, cutting across the hundred yards between them.

As Ed wonders if he can still clean up the spilled coffee, you wake up.

The Bedroom Mirror
Anne Fox

In forty-five minutes, Emil, your new life. Check your tie, blue-on-blue silk, smooth under your finger. Secure the stickpin, the chip of diamond a point of morning light. Good, no tremble in the hand. Remember, it was not for Esther to ask and not for you to promise. It was a good life the two of you had. Now, no more wondering—you'll never know why she asked.

Trim the moustache. The feather-edge dust floats into your hand. Yes, you are a lucky man.

Put on your coat. A fine figure you cut—tall, thin, no stoop. No droopy eyelids. No floppy cheeks. No veins breaking under the skin. Still your own teeth. Yes, smile. You have the right. Tell yourself again.

Helen's watch on your wrist, platinum and guaranteed for a lifetime. You laughed. Whose lifetime? Helen didn't laugh. She put it in your hand, folded her fingers over yours. Esther's gold watch is already under the handkerchiefs in the drawer, the inscription—Esther to Emil—cut into the heart of gold forever. Forever? It will stop ticking.

Whisk the shoulders. The pinstripe, a perfect fit. The handkerchief points exactly so in the breast pocket. Check the fingernails.

Esther watches from her filigree-framed photograph on the dresser, her smile mysterious. Don't forget the eyebrows.

'John L Lewis eyebrows,' Esther called them.

'Your eyebrows—striking with your white hair,' Helen said and ran her finger over them.

Your promise to Esther shattered at Helen's touch.

Take a good look. Admit it, you're a vain man. You learned long ago about silk ties and Paco Rabanne. They don't tailor-make sackcloth and ashes.

Smooth back your hair. The hat has to fit perfectly. Esther always liked you in a hat. She bought you every kind and showed you off. Remember the feel of her arm linked in yours, the lightness of her hand at your elbow?

Helen is a good-looking woman. Your friends wink—lightning strikes twice.

Look at Esther's eyes in the photograph. You shake your head. Why that question whispered, her cold hand pressing yours? You still wonder about the wilderness of your promise.

'No, of course not, my darling. I never will.'

And then Helen, illuminating a dark and lonely place. The end of the world didn't come, did it?

Put on your hat, nudge the brim. Esther's eyes follow you around the room. She sees you feel in your pocket for your wallet, your keys, the new wedding ring. She sees your hand touch the frame. She doesn't know it's for the last time.

But you know it must be for the last time, don't you, Emil?

Take the photo; put it with the gold watch. Yes, put the past in the darkness of the drawer under the handkerchiefs along with the promise—an old, fragile promise.

Time to go. Tip your hat to the mirror and walk out the door.

Helen is waiting.

HOME STRANGE HOME
Diandra Linnemann

ALL it takes is a blink of your eye.

You have never been to this place before. You are not even sure how you got here. The couch is strangely familiar, its worn upholstery fuzzy with white cat hair. You are sure you have never owned a red couch.

The cats are watching you. Their faces show disappointment. It's the way cats view the world. The room is quiet; not even the ticking of a clock disturbs the silence. Outside the huge window, trees bend in the breeze.

Why are you missing the ticking of a clock?

A closer look at yourself—black pants, black t-shirt. You would never wear anything like this, or would you? Who are you?

Best be careful. You put aside the novel you hold in your lap. Do not look at the cover. The pages tucked under your left thumb indicate you have read far, yet you have no idea what the story is about. Is it fiction, non-fiction? Might be a VCR manual—no, too many pages for that. You put it down on the table next to an empty coffee-stained cup. The faint lipstick smudges are a funny colour, way too bright, surely not yours.

A fragment of memory flashes—a meadow, laughing children. Sepia-coloured memories. Is this something you experienced or saw in a movie? The children's faces make you happy and sad at the same time.

One of the cats jumps down from the windowsill, struts up to you and rubs itself against your leg. Immediately your pants are covered in cat hair. They look better, more familiar, this way. You bend down to pet the cat's head. It hisses and hides under the cupboard.

The door to what must be the living room opens and a strange man looks at you quizzically. You breathe a sigh of relief. Surely everything will fall into place. It's all just a misunder—

'Darling, are you ready? My parents are expecting us for dinner.'

'I…uh, I must have forgotten the time.' What else is there to say?

He is wearing dark blue pants and a striped shirt, no tie. You realize you are more familiar with him wearing a tie. So he is an office guy. Part of your brain has already accepted this madness and is playing along.

Another part has curled up in a corner of your mind. You smile, pick up the coffee cup and follow him.

The flat is tidy. You enter the hallway and see an open door leading into the kitchen. You place the cup in the sink. The details can be figured out later.

'You don't intend to go like that?'

His question surprises you. What's wrong with your clothes? Since you cannot ask him without shattering this fragile reality, you smile and shake your head.

'Give me a minute to change.'

'Hurry, we're late!' He nods in the direction of a closed door. When you open it, you find yourself standing in the master bedroom.

It smells of sleep, warm sheets and faintly of love. You don't remember a thing.

The laughing children flash through your mind. You shake your head, ridding yourself of what may be a dream, or a memory.

One of the wardrobe doors is slightly cracked open and something yellow and frilly spills out of it. You grab the nearest thing—a long mauve skirt and a matching white blouse. It looks like a church outfit. Do you go to church regularly? No way of knowing. You are running out of time so you change quickly and grab a comb from the dresser to run through your curls. Your hair is longer than you expect. You put the comb down and avoid looking into the mirror. You're afraid of who you are, who you have become.

'I'm ready, let's go.'

The man smiles, gives you a peck on the cheek. 'You look lovely.'

Together you descend the stairs. You wonder what this life has in store for you.

The Bridge over the River Illias
Robert Lee Frazier

An owl screeches in the distance and you brace your legs in your horse's stirrups, reminding yourself that you stopped believing old wives' tales long ago.

A voice rings out. You turn from contemplating the flight of the owl to the stiff form of the Sergeant-at-arms, Neglis. Grey at the temples, he is still tough as nails. Neglis has seen close to twice as many winters as you but keeps up, step for step, with the young recruits in your company.

'Captain Belaro, the advance scouts have reported back. The road is clear from here to the bridge.'

You let out a sigh of relief. The bridge. The reason you are here. The reason you received your commission a full year before you should have, received it from the governor himself.

You nod to the sergeant and he gets the company moving again. Most are slow to get up. A corporal starts shouting for them to get back into ranks.

Your horse whinnies and snorts loudly. You start out on the road knowing it's good for the troops to see you lead, but secretly you are just trying to keep your horse upwind, away from the smell of fear.

Nightfall approaches and your troops are ensconced in their field tents or staffing guard positions along the steep banks of the River Illias. The men are tired. Between the three day march and the work of building improvised defences, they no longer smell of fear, just exhaustion.

When you came upon the lonely little frontier footbridge this morning, the Corporal called it a dump. Neither you, nor Sergeant Neglis, reprimanded him. Secretly you agreed.

Then, while the troops were busy, you took time to wander out onto the bridge, a construction of nothing more than wooden planks and double braided ropes. Thinking it probably couldn't hold the weight of a single horse and rider, you began questioning the governor's decision. Why bother sending a company out here? Intelligence from across the border indicated that the enemy was massing farther south, preparing for an all-out assault near the town of Kalis where the river could easily be crossed.

The sun dips below the trees. You dine in your tent alone. You are still thinking about the intelligence reports when Sergeant Neglis sticks his head inside your tent.

'Excuse me sir, will you please step out here for a moment?'

You follow him out and stare in surprise across the river at the huge number of bonfires and the growing sound of men, horses and war machines.

Others of the company gather in silence, listening. You recognize one sound amongst the growing clamour, your horse.

It is whinnying and snorting loudly. As the light of day dims you look around at the young recruits and wonder how long they can possibly hold out—after you have mounted up and fled.

MARATHON TO PERFECTION
Margaret Gracie

IT begins with praise. Random. Parcelled out. A few words for a pretty drawing. Strangers commenting on your dress, your hair, the way you always say please and thank you. A feeling sprouts inside—warm, moist, the opposite of hunger. You feel closer to the sky.

Praise becomes your drug of choice. You seek it out from everyone: neighbours, teachers, family and friends. You listen carefully for signs of displeasure. Take note. Change your behaviour by degrees; approval is your true north. Remember to take better care of your clothes, brush your hair, polish your shoes, clean your teeth, complete your homework, and feed the dog. You even do the dishes without being asked, tidy your room, help with the chores, ask your mother how her day has been, and buy your friends birthday gifts they don't yet know they need.

In adulthood, you continue your quest. There are more ways to fail. You must draw on hidden reserves. Get accepted into the best school, fulfil your boyfriends' needs, take less, give more, work harder, and complain only when absolutely necessary. You sew, cook, get a good job, get married without making a fuss, plan vacations, do the gardening, clean the house, read baby books before you get pregnant, take the right tests, eat only the healthiest food, opt for natural childbirth and only agree to the epidural when the doctor says you should. You survive on three hours sleep, feed and change the baby without forgetting your husband, have sex even when bloated and raw, pamper, discipline, show you care without smothering, go to junior recitals and little league games, cheer, empathize, buy ice-cream cones, give baths, learn to leave the bathroom door unlocked when it's your turn, never mention your fatigue, hide your disappointment, swallow your feelings of loss—youth, freedom, time.

The years pass and you never feel as if you have arrived. The goalpost constantly moves then disintegrates before you have a chance to memorize where it was; yet you know it exists because everyone else seems to measure you up against it.

You are always falling short. One wrong word. A small misdeed. Your son says he hates you. Your husband leaves. Your boss stops smiling at you. Your friends are too busy with their own lives to pick up the phone.

You would let it all fall away, this need for praise, but then you'd have nothing. So instead you hold on. You focus on the few inches in front of you, the next step, and you tell yourself to try harder.

LILY
Hettie Ashwin

I F you saw her in the daylight you'd probably say she was old. Old and ugly. You might even wince a little, a small screwing up of your nose and the slight shrug of your shoulders. No one could blame you and there would be no need to feel guilty. Because, after all, she is old and she is ugly. Everyone thought so; you were just going that one step further.

But she is a night owl. A person who only lives in the shadows of darkness. A person who, once the sun has set, comes alive. You've seen her before at the bar—or others just like her—and your heart beat a little faster. The makeup, fancy clothes and witty talk. Attracted like a moth to a flame, you loved them and if you were honest with yourself, you wanted to be just like them.

Lily sat at the coffee table and leaned a little to the right. She rummaged around in her handbag—the same handbag she had last night when you watched her swaying to the music, gin in hand—and found a cigarette. It was bent and she carefully straightened it before putting it to her lips. She couldn't see you but you figured she knew you were there, at the table to her right, watching behind your dark sunglasses. At one point, Lily turned and looked at you, stared straight into your eyes. She waited a second or two then turned and the waiter came to her rescue with a lighter. It was like she had been waiting all her life for that one cigarette. That one deep drag that reached deep into her body and excited her will to live. You could almost taste the smoke as she exhaled and sat back. You licked your lips in expectation.

She had style. A certain way she dressed and carried herself. You tried to copy her many times. Emulating her in front of your mirror at home, that dress, the handbag, the sunglasses, and the hat. It was what you wanted. You only had to admit it. You only had to let go of the past, embrace the new you. At night Lily was wonderful. At night she came alive.

Your life seemed, in comparison, very ordinary. No sequins for you. Mother and Father, with their high expectations, had set you on a path for ordinary and never wavered in their expressions of satisfaction at the way you had turned out. Mother was a little more understanding than father and you often wanted to confide in her, but you never did, and she remained a childhood memory of soft cardigans and Channel No. 5 long after you had left home. Nothing was ever said, the words never spoken and the home fire continued to burn in fake ignorance.

Lily sat back and basked in the morning sun, a delicate flower trying to rejuvenate in the light. She was a creature of habit and you watched her with a fascination bordering on obsession: the way she sipped her morning coffee; the paper she read, skipping over the words and just looking at the pictures; her habit of disappearing at 10 am and not re-emerging until nightfall. It was quite a thrill to rifle through her mail as she slept, pawing over her bills, her letters from friends and her junk subscriptions. Empowered, you experienced a sort of strength never felt before and it excited you. It gave you courage.

The first night she spoke to you it almost went horribly wrong. You gagged on the words, stammered, stuttered and feigned a sore throat. How understanding she was. How sympathetic when she touched your hand. Lily's hand wasn't young. It wasn't smooth but wrinkled and old. Its veins stuck out and the knuckles were arthritic. But it was beautiful to you. You bought her a drink and she commented on your clothes. You survived on her remarks for weeks, alone in your one room apartment.

Now, Lily turned again and smiled, beckoning you over.

'Me?' you said, and touched your neck in a feminine delicate way. She nodded and called for a second cup.

So many times you had imagined this moment. Lily patted the spare seat and cleared away the morning paper.

'Coffee?' A nod sufficed as the simplest of words seemed stuck in your throat. She smiled at you and that smile melted your trepidation.

You placed your handbag on the table and crossed your legs, letting the left fall languidly at an angle over the right, just like Jackie O. It was a practised movement but it made them look so slender, so chic and it felt right. Lily sucked her bottom lip as she watched your every move. Was it a test? Did she see something, a longing, a desire?

'Don't try too hard, it will come naturally,' she said, picking at a stray thread on the tablecloth. You nodded again and smiled.

'What is your name?'

'Edwar—' you said, catching yourself. 'Catherine.'

Lily patted your hand, the same caring gesture of understanding from the other night.

It would be the start of something. Something that could take your breath away. Something that could be called love. It might be more than that as she guides you through the metamorphosis. From the day to the night. From trousers to frocks.

From Edward to Catherine.

AT THE EDGE OF THE MATTRESS
Annemaria Cooper

YOU lie at the edge of the mattress, defeated, foetal. Hanging on, suspended in the sorrow of darkness. Heavy and pendulous, the teardrop won't wait. It falls onto the cotton. You hold your breath. He can't know you're awake. Did he hear it fall?

Your nose is running but you can't reach for a tissue. That will tell him you're awake. From the pit of your stomach you control the *faux* sleep. Your lips are dry, a cork is swelling in your throat, but you are in control. You have to be. He isn't asleep yet.

He has decided who your friends are—it isn't a big decision to make. He decides what you eat, what you wear. He's been controlling you since the day you met. *You know.* There is only your basic instinct of survival, but it all depends on breathing.

Your head is pounding. Blood is rushing. Tears are pooling, ready to fall. How long can you lie with your face against wet cloth? You pray. *Please let him sleep.* Eventually, the pool floods over and finds a valley between plumped cheek and nostril. It misses your mouth as it slithers along its path.

You cough, act as if it's a pattern of sleep, and reach for a tissue. Desperate not to waken the argument—the one he started and you could not fight—your actions are measured. Your fingers brush the tissue, pulling slowly. You hear the paper slide from its box as you hold your breath. Will one noise alert him, two soft noises? You wipe, soak and mop.

You are aching to move, fearing the edge. Muscles volunteer to twitch a puffy eyelid. How heavy they feel when you blink in the darkness. Toes move, slightly stroking the sheet, soothing and comforting in an infantile way while all the time you are thinking, *please don't let him know I'm awake.* You press your lips to silence your thoughts.

Beneath the Christmas decorations in the hall cupboard there is a sports bag; the just-in-case solution. You think of the contents. Spare clothes, toiletries, and a picture of a family, your family, once happy, naïve, the future then unknown. If courage found its way to you, would it find its way to them? It's been four years since you hid that bag. You smile as a bizarre thought enters your head. *What else is packed?*

You didn't escape then, did you? You can't escape now. He has taken to the mattresses. All you can do is hold on to the edge and control your breathing, quiet, safe, and alive.

THAT LOVING FEELING
Sharon Birch

YOU don't know what to do. Everything he does irritates you and grates on your nerves. You hate yourself for being so mean, for responding with nastiness, but you can't seem to help it. You try to take it back, so you smile at him.

You feel sorry for him, for the situation. Sympathy makes you make love to him. He thinks that it's all right now and his eagerness makes your guilt rise like bile.

You try to keep it light and the next day you crack some jokes and smile at him again. Inside, the pounding headache that is your life throbs louder. You have that sickly migraine feeling that won't go away with two aspirin.

You love him. Of course you do. But what happened to the spark, the fire in your belly? That flame of passion that filled your head? Where did it all go?

You buy him a gift. You tell him you love him. You try to create the tingle factor that was once all you lived for. Life has somehow got in the way. Mundane shopping on a bank holiday. Sweeping up the front path on a sunny Sunday. Seeing aged relatives on any other day. It all takes you away from him, his presence. You don't want to spend any more time with him than you have to because there is nothing left to say. And yet, you still try. You suggest going out for the night. At least you can mingle with the crowd and pretend. He doesn't want that. He wants you, on your own.

You decide, finally, you just don't want him. It's done. You make something up to throw back at him when he asks, in tears, why you are leaving. You know it's not the truth but you say it anyway. You tell him it has eaten away at you like a worm in apple. You try to make it your fault and say that you know he is no longer happy with you.

He asks again, *why*? You take a deep breath and respond.
For you, for her.

You tell him it is so he can be with this other woman. She's his boss and they spend a lot of time together, so it fits. You remember the late nights he has spent working away. You try to act jealous but know it's just an excuse, a ready-made meal of distasteful lies that will leave a sour taste once you've gone. But, knowing it's not real, you say it anyway. A reason when you haven't a real one. All you want to do is to be alone, to be where he is not.

And then he asks. He asks you how you *knew*.

You didn't. *You made it up.*

And in that moment you realise, it was his fault after all.

To Light a Candle
Heidi Gilhooly

A glimpse. That's all it takes to remind you, to take you back. Sitting at a window table at the café, you see him. The tall, lean stature. The straight nose and full lips that you can imagine curling into a smile that spreads right into his dark eyes. The skin the shade of the darkest granite.

You frown, glance at your papers and look up again. The man is gone. But instead of getting up to leave, you order another coffee.

Your thoughts travel back five years, to a rainy April morning when you were drinking your first cup of coffee of the day. You were in an African country known for its natural beauty and political unrest. You had travelled there with *Glamorous* to prepare a swimwear promotion. Somewhat hung-over, you had little interest in the other occupants of the hotel restaurant. Suddenly, a man shouted in English.

'Put your hands up in the air!'

You were faced by three masked men.

'Yes. You too, lady,' he added pointing a rifle at you.

You remember raising your hands and slowly getting up to stand when instructed to do so. The room was eerily silent as you and your fellow hotel guests realised your lives depended on not making any wrong moves. Even the irritating American woman from CNN stopped her incessant chatter.

You were led to a spacious ballroom that was decked with cane furniture and lively African prints. The heavy draped curtains were drawn and remained so for the next two days and nights.

There were five of you: the irritating CNN woman, a Danish businessman, an Australian backpacker waiting to join an excursion, a Sudanese student, and you. Although concerned for your own safety, you remember your relief that at least 'your girls' were in their rooms sorting out their hair and make up for the shoot.

Once your eyes grew accustomed to the lack of light, you observed that the three hostage takers wore masks. You took this as a good sign. They wanted to protect their identities. They were not intent on killing.

'You cannot just take the law into your own hands, that's anarchy!' The CNN woman, having found her voice again, challenged the men.

'So, what's so bad about that when you compare it to what is being done to us in the name of our government,' said the man with the smooth hands and long fingers. He spoke excellent English.

'You should use peaceful means,' the CNN woman continued. 'Get the support of western governments.'

Smooth Hands translated the comment to his colleagues. All three of them laughed, one wiped his eyes with the back of his wrinkled hand.

'You, madam, have a sense of humour,' Smooth Hands said. But you noticed the hardening of his voice when he explained what was to happen. Demands would need to be met. He pointed his gun at each of you in turn.

'You,' he said. 'It could be you. If our requests are ignored, one of you will be shot tomorrow morning.'

You felt sick, scared for your life. You were not ready to die. Despite not considering yourself religious you spent the rest of the day in silent prayer. You pleaded with all the gods you could think of to save you and your companions. Although you had hardly spoken with the others, your sense of fairness insisted that your prayers include those who shared your fate.

You refused the food that was brought in. You remember concentrating on the sounds surrounding you in a desperate search for a word or two that would make sense.

You knew it was evening when the hostage takers brought in a television set to watch the evening news. It was tuned to an English language channel and you were confronted with images of the hotel and your distraught girls crying on camera.

After your escorted visit to the toilet, the lights were dimmed. You pulled a blanket over your shoulders and settled on the cane sofa. That's when you noticed that the Sudanese student was staring at you. Instead of settling himself for the night, he crossed the room to approach you.

'I am Matthew,' he introduced himself. 'I can see that you are troubled.'

'Well that's bleeding obvious,' you said more strongly than intended. 'Have you not noticed that we've been taken hostage and may be killed?'

Matthew looked at you. He bowed his head to take his leave, but you reached out your hand to stop him. You apologised for your outburst, explained that the pressure was getting to you.

He stayed there that night, sharing your sofa. You spoke about your life in London, your work for *Glamorous*. Pointing at your wedding ring, he asked about your husband. Haltingly, you explained that you'd been married for five years. You no longer had anything in common with your husband, but you were too busy to think about it.

He spoke about his role as the eldest son of a family with ten children. He smiled at your question about his Christian sounding first name by declaring himself a Catholic from Southern Sudan. His family were wealthy by Sudanese standards, thus he was able to continue his education after his graduation from the University of Khartoum. He was on his way to the United States to take up a scholarship for his PhD studies. You said something about admiring him to which he responded that he did not understand your meaning.

You must have slept a little that night as you remember the feeling of nausea when your memory jolted you back to reality. You raised your head, realising it had been resting on Matthew's shoulder. He smiled at you reassuringly, his perfect white teeth glistening in the dark room.

Smooth Hands spoke on the telephone once again. You still remember his stern voice. A moment after replacing the receiver, he uttered one word. At this, Wrinkled Hands got up and pointed his rifle at the Dane. You felt like screaming, like getting up and jumping at the hostage taker. The backpacker rose and pleaded with Smooth Hands, attempting to appeal to his respect for life. You saw the look of fear on the Dane's face.

Moments after the Dane was led from the room, you heard a shot. The CNN woman threw herself on the floor, the backpacker started to cry, you observed tears running down his sun streaked face like rivulets after a heavy rain. Matthew held you in his arms, wiping away your tears.

You felt stifled that day, not only by the intense heat, but also by the atmosphere in the room. Afterwards, you wrote in your notebook about fear and confusion, but even now you're not sure whether these were the right words.

The scenario with the television and telephone was repeated that evening. News reports speculated about the shooting of a hostage; no body was found. Your heart missed a beat when Smooth Hands turned towards you after the telephone call.

Again, he pointed his gun at each of you in turn. 'One of you will be shot in the morning if our demands are not met.'

You let out a muffled cry, by now the room was full of sobbing and pleading. Only Matthew remained quiet, sitting on the cane sofa.

You would never forget that night, never forget sitting there with Matthew, wrapped up in a blanket—the pattern of which you could still trace today. Nor would you forget the intensity of realising that more than anything you wanted to live. There were so many things you wanted to do, so many dreams pushed away until later. Faced with the prospect of there not being a later, you wanted to grab life in your hands.

You tried to ask Matthew about his life. Did he have a girlfriend, someone special? He seemed bemused and talked about his affairs being settled.

He was interested in you. What were you going to do when you got home? Did you enjoy your work as a fashion editor? You told him you were not going back to your old life. You were going to hunt down these murderous people. You were going to ensure that they were convicted for you believed in justice.

He smiled at you, but questioned what justice meant. He said that perhaps these men believed they were freedom fighters, or whatever people who fought for their ideas were called in your world. He talked about Nelson Mandela who'd been convicted of rebelling against a legitimate government. In years to come these men may be seen as having fought for a just cause.

You started to cry. You did not want to think about these issues. But you knew that whatever happened in the morning, you could not go back.

'What can I do?' you sobbed.

Matthew told you about a sign he'd seen in Tanzania, near the Olduvai Gorge, that read:

It is better to light a candle than to complain about the darkness.

He said that in his life he always tried to do what he could to serve God and his country. That way he would be ready to leave when his time came. He would leave knowing that he had lived life to the full.

You cried yourself to sleep that night. Afterwards, you often wondered about the bizarre situation when you were comforted by a man whose world was so different from yours.

You remember Smooth Hands' telephone call that morning, his short commands and how Wrinkled Hands' rifle pointed at Matthew.

'You,' the order was issued. 'Our demands have not been met, so you are going to die.'

You remember kissing Matthew's clammy cheek before he was led out of the room. You can still recall the strong squeeze of his hand. The single shot. You remember the CNN woman and the backpacker sitting together, talking together, crying.

You remember the noise of helicopters later that day. The gunfire. The hostage takers' frantic shouting. The CNN woman seeking shelter under a table, the backpacker throwing his sleeping bag over her as if to create a barrier, a shelter. The hostage takers pulling the drapes aside and blinding you with the bright sunshine before breaking the window and running out. The sounds and smells of the African day bursting in and intoxicating you with life.

You remember the police, and someone wrapping you in a blanket and leading you out past the press photographers and journalists.

You remember stepping over the hostage takers' blood-stained bodies. Their unmasked faces contorted in pain.

The bodies of the Dane and Matthew were never found, and you remain enraged about speculation that they were part of the gang.

After your return to London, you handed in your notice to *Glamorous* and started divorce proceedings. Thus set free, you joined a worldwide development agency and enrolled on a course in international relations. Today you are presenting a documentary celebrating the independence of the Republic of South Sudan, which you produced together with Angela, the CNN woman whom you now call your friend.

You close your laptop and take a deep breath before sliding it into your bag. No wonder your mind is playing tricks today.

Casting one last look out the window, you sling the bag onto your shoulder and head for the conference centre.

ODDS
Sarah Evans

IT is odd, being you.

Your steam-smeared image gazes back from the bathroom mirror as you reflect. A typical ejaculate contains ten million spermatozoa, once you've excluded the dead, the malformed and those swimming backwards. You only ever had a one in ten million chance. And that's before you think it might not have been the right time of month, or she might've been on the Pill, or they might not have been in the mood. More than half of zygotes self-abort anyway.

The odds are against you.

'You in there for the night, Caro?' your brother calls. You don't grace him with an answer.

Instead, you slant your head one way then the other, taking in the fullness of your lips and wondering if the colour is too glossy bright. Your lined, mascaraed, blue-shadowed eyes narrow in scrutiny. You think how strange it is that you only ever see your face in reflection, slightly warped and dimmed, somewhat posed and watchful.

The doorbell chimes. Time, which seemed as foamed up as the scented bubbles slopping over the bath you lingered in earlier, pricks to nothing.

'Just a minute,' you shout. Details can't be scrimped: a feathering of silvery dust across your blushed cheekbones; an extra, good-luck spray of *Pure Poison*; a final head twist while your toes tighten round the rim of the bath as you check the size of your bum in your condom tight dress.

Odds of fatally slipping in bath or shower: one in 2,232. Ballerina-ing on the enamelled edge must up them.

You slip your nylon covered feet into your red, spike-heeled shoes with criss-crossed straps and sparkle. They pinch. You unlock the door.

Your hips movie-star sway down the stairs. You can hear Marlene in the kitchen and your mum asking if she'd like a cup of tea.

'No thanks, Mrs Dawson.' Marlene is on her best behaviour, but not for long.

At the bus-stop, the wind freezes through your silk-thin layers and chest-folded arms. The two of you keep warm on chatter, flowing more from Marlene than you and all of it is vital, belly-ache funny, and none of it will you remember because it's not the words that matter, but the bubbling, included-ness. You're no longer odd on your own.

In a college of 571, and the two of you doing different subjects, the chances of her being your friend are low. You got lucky.

The bus arrives fifteen minutes late and you can see another one coming up behind. *Bleeding typical*...according to that probability distribution you drew carefully in double maths.

The odds of being killed on a five mile bus journey are one in 500,000,000. You read that online. You like collecting oddities. Your bus journey is only a mile and a half.

Each of you pushes open a double door, pressing it back into the fug of warmth and noise.

'What you having?' you shout, though you know the answer.

The chances of the barman asking for ID are minimal. No one ever has, but it doesn't stop your heart thumping to your throat as you practice your most brazen smile. You're glad to get the gangling lad who looks pre-teen and does no more than repeat your order: two cider and blacks.

The pub is shoulder-shoving packed so it's against all expectation that you find two high stools in a corner from where you perch like exotic parrots, pivoting your heads to survey the scene.

'Tonight's the night,' Marlene insists. She's like your mother with a lottery ticket. *It could be you.*

'There's a formula,' you shout above the roar. 'For dating.'

'Get on with you,' she says and laughs.

'No seriously. I worked it out.' During double maths.

'Go on then, genius girl.'

The odds of finding out your child is a genius are one in 250. So you read.

'The formula is *P* times a quarter times point two all divided by five.' You trace it out on the narrow ledge behind you.

$$[(P \times 0.25) \times 0.2] / 5$$

'*P* is the number of initial chat-ups,' you explain.

'Wha-at?' Marlene graces you with a dopey grin and her eyes are like a lighthouse beam scanning round the sawdust space. Lads cluster at the terracotta pillars that support arches of flaking brick. They're drinking, acting loud, jostling, talking footy and maybe girls. Girls huddle in twos and threes and gaggles. There are couples, and two by twos, looking smug.

'Suppose you meet someone,' you say. 'Like someone here comes over to chat you up.'

'Uh huh.'

You're not sure Marlene is listening as she sips her drink and rocks her stool backwards on two legs, her elbows back against the ledge, her body sequinned, sleek and sexy.

'So he's one of the *Ps*.'

'The peas?'

The two of you giggle. The alcohol has straight-lined to your head and is busily killing off brain cells.

'One of those you happen to meet. Like him.' You gesture over at a lad who's staring at Marlene from under chaotic eyebrows.

'Him? No way.'

'Well, exactly. For each new acquaintance you multiply by a quarter for initial attraction.'

'One in four? You're kidding, right?'

You glance round. Even in the dim light and through the haze of alcohol, the lanky limbs and acned faces don't yell Jude Law. The best of them are already paired and you wonder if your formula should take that into account.

'Well, let's just say.' The maths are dreary enough already. 'Let's say if four lads came up to say *hi*, there'd be one you don't run screaming from.'

'Oh-*Kaay*.'

'So you get talking and what's the chance you'll swap phone numbers? That's the naught point two. One in five.'

'Give one in five my number? No way.'

'No. One in five times a quarter. Because you have to have fancied him first. So now we're at...' The math isn't difficult. At least it wouldn't be if your head wasn't buzzing. 'One in twenty. Five per cent.'

'Twenty? There are not twenty lads I fancy here.' She's lost the thread. You press on regardless. It all made perfect sense in double maths at 3pm this afternoon.

'Then, even if you swap numbers, he might not call, or you might change your mind. That's another one in five. So now you're down to one per cent. For every hundred lads who try the chat-up thing only one will make it to a date.'

You picture getting a hundred lads to form an orderly queue and walk by, with you sorting them, until you're left with one, the perfect one.

'You know your problem?' she says, her words choking through laughter. 'You think too much.'

Marlene got lucky. She didn't have to wait for four; she is head-together giggling with the first. Only a one in four chance of that. And the chance you'll fancy his mate as well is one in four times one in four, which is one in sixteen. So it isn't surprising that you don't. But you smile as if to say *maybe*. It's too early to head home. It's too early for Marlene to want to be alone with Tony and she'd be pissed at you if you screw this up for her.

She has the better of the two. The odds of that are pretty much one hundred per cent.

Ian, yours is called. Except that he isn't yours because he has bad skin and dandruff and he's fishing-rod thin and, in your strappy heels, you're taller. His jacket is washed-out, fraying denim.

All of which is superficial; perhaps you're a superficial person.

'So what do you do?' Ian shouts over the jukebox, which is belting out *Live Like We're Dying*.

'College,' you say, though earlier you overheard Marlene side-step the question and say something vague and flirty and suggestive. Something that would sound stupid coming from you. Besides, you don't want to suggest anything to Ian.

'A levels,' you add so he doesn't think you're into hairdressing or childcare. 'Biology and maths. And further maths. You?'

'Apprentice,' he says. 'Plumber.'

'Oh.' You could say that sounds interesting, except it doesn't. Or that you've heard plumbers make more money than graduates. But that sounds condescending or money-grabbing or something.

Your eyes scan round the dim-lit expanse as you try to make out some of the one in four lads you might have fancied. Only one in four also assumes they fancy you.

Marlene was right. One in four is way too many.

Three rounds and lots of laughter later, Marlene and Tony are standing hip to hip, and you are tapping your foot and mouthing to the music.

Tony whispers to Marlene. She turns your way and you catch the smell of blackcurrant. You make out the words *party* and *you've got to come* and *wheels.*

'Wheels? But he's been drinking.'

'Low alcohol lager.'

You wonder what the odds are of that being true.

The chance of dying in a car accident is one in 18,174. You wonder how much it notches up when the driver is young, male and quite probably somewhat pissed.

'You've got to come. What if he's an axe murderer?' Marlene whisper-shouts.

Coincidentally, the odds of being murdered are one in 18,291. Odds of getting away with murder: two to one. Odds of Marlene no longer being your friend if you start to be a bore? You're not about to find out.

You strap yourself into the backseat, which smells of leather and sweaty socks, and you wonder how loudly you could scream if he has an axe.

The car heads down the high street, past the undertakers on the corner to the major roundabout. It turns left onto a B road, then right onto an unnumbered one, then left, then straight ahead until you don't know where you are. Tony has his hand on Marlene's thigh. He drives one handed and you wish that he'd use two. Your hand is palm down on the sweaty leather and Ian reaches across to place his hand over yours. You should slide yours away, but you don't.

Just like you should worry at the way that 18,000 is whittling down, but actually you're not. The world is slipping by and beneath the headlights the road is glittered by frost, and the trees bend over the road like a rose arch. The car glides smoothly into the bends, then rises to a peak—the black outline of trees on the horizon forming a lacy trim—before it plunges down.

But then the odds change.

You're slammed back into the leather—knowing that a moment earlier you were hurtling forward—as the car comes to a face-slap stop. Someone's scream is echoing in your ears. The seat belt has left a bruising stripe across your chest and your stomach's sick and your breath lost. Tony is slumped forward and Marlene's face, reflected in the moonlight, is white beneath her blusher. Ian's fingernails are embedded into your palm.

'Shit!' Ian says. 'Shit!' And then an hour-long minute later, 'You alright?' Except it isn't clear who he is asking.

It is quiet and still and no one breathes. You think how the highest cause of death for teenage boys is smashing up cars.

Smoke is rising in a grey plume from the crumpled front and your seat is sloping sideways and the silhouetted trees are too close. Your eyes catch a flash of red. You smell the metal of blood and the reek of burning rubber. Someone groans. Marlene moves in slow motion, her hand reaching out and you can see the instinctive recoil, like some of the girls in biology practical, though you have never minded the dead rats. *Oh my God, oh my God, oh my God* is looping through your mind, like the refrain of a catchy song.

You don't believe in God.

Someone groans again, a deep-throated rumble, and it could be you. Except it isn't.

Slowly Tony's shoulders start to shift and you see how the airbag has inflated. The red is only his tie and you realise you've bitten your lip. You laugh, but not because it's funny.

'Shit!' Tony says it now, as his fist disappears into the white billow of the airbag.

The urge to throw up tremors through you. You open the door until it jambs. One leg slithers out and then the other. Your heel keeps sinking downwards and your ankle twists. Your legs are weak and trembly. Those heels were always too bloody high.

The air is frostbite cold and as you feel your way round the car the metal sticks to your fingers. Ian is behind and then in front and reaching out a hand to pull you up the bank. You bend forward and retch. You taste blackcurrant mixed with stomach acid.

You spit then stand back straight and shiver. Ian slips his jacket over your shoulders and his hand round your waist. In the dark you can't see his acne, which is only skin deep anyway. You hear Marlene shouting, and Tony shouting louder. You can't make out the words, just the furious shape of them. You think he's probably not one of the one in five.

Ian pulls you closer. 'You alright Caro?' he asks. Your head drops like a stone onto his shoulder and you keep your eyes open. The sky is patterned with stars, much brighter than they ever are in town, as if someone's turned the level up. You trace the familiar forms, though the names of constellations seem to have jolted from your brain. The road is a silver ribbon and the white bark of the beech trees glints in the moonlight.

And you are just a girl, standing with goosebump arms, heart and stomach settling, weighed down beneath a denim jacket. A girl suspended in the frozen glory of the night.

You think how odd it is that you are here, and you are you.

GONNAGETYA
Meriah L Crawford

Yᴏᴜ'ʀᴇ leaving your hotel room, mind on dinner and drinks in the restaurant downstairs, when two kids burst out of the room across the hall. A girl is fast on the heels of a young boy. As he runs, screaming, the girl shouts after him.

'Gonnagetya, gonnagetya, gonnagetya, little pus head!'

Thirty feet down the hall, he stumbles and she catches up with him. What do you do? Do you just stand there watching, doing nothing as she drags him by the hair, back the way they came?

The boy screams, 'Hurtee, hurtee! Lizzie, hurtee!' The girl's pretty pixie face twists in a cruel, triumphant smile.

Do you try to stop her? She's hurting him, but she's just a little girl. Her pale blonde hair is in pigtails, her feet in pink flip-flops, and the rest of her is dressed in red shorts and a faded Pooh t-shirt. She looks far too sweet, too delicate to do much harm.

The boy, blond and blue-eyed, is dressed all in blue. His wet t-shirt, with its lopsided Superman logo, clings to his bony chest. He tries to twist away, and she swings around and punches him on the arm, making him howl.

His pain makes you flinch, and your heart pounds. Someone should make her stop, but who—you? What if she screams out for help and someone comes running and accuses *you* of abuse? It could happen. And if it did? You'd be screwed.

'Momma's gonna whup your ass but good,' the little girl says, still dragging him. Now that changes things a bit. *That* you've got to stop.

But wait, she's his mother. And parents have a right to discipline their kids, don't they?

Well, sure, but deep down you believe any competent parent can control, raise and nurture a child without any violent acts. You view spanking as archaic, cruel and unnecessary.

It occurs to you that you could ask the little girl what her brother's done to justify such treatment. But by the time you turn to ask the question, you see their room door just clicking shut, muffling the little boy's terrified cries. Another voice—booming, female—joins in, expressing anger through the thin hotel walls.

Still you stand there, just outside your own hotel room, paralysed by uncertainty. You know you must act, but you wait for your brain to kick in and tell you how.

Then you hear a crack, and you know that sweet little boy just got smacked across the face. His cries stop instantly.

How hard do you have to hit a little boy to make him *stop* screaming? How many times has he been hit before in his short life? What kind of a monster would do such a thing?

You consider knocking on the door, demanding to know what's happening to the poor boy. But it's a ridiculous thought. You know you don't have it in you—and even if you did, what would you say? What can you say to a woman who's abusing her child?

Finally, you unfreeze. You turn, slide your card through the door lock, and then stride to the phone. You hesitate for a moment, but decide to call the front desk. If you tell them, it'll be their problem.

A young woman answers. She listens to your little tale and asks what you want her to do about it. The implication is clear. She wants no part of it, wonders why you're bothering her with what's clearly a personal problem. You wish for a moment that you could just turn and leave the room, go to dinner and have a stiff drink.

Instead, you urge her to take steps, though you're vague about what those steps should be. Eventually, she agrees to look into it.

Relieved that you've done your duty, handed off the responsibility, you leave your room again, thinking of the tall, cold drink that will shortly be in your hands.

You take a few steps toward the elevator and are almost opposite their room when you hear a phone ring. You hear murmurs and then the phone slams down and the bellowing resumes. There's another crack and the boy screams again.

You turn on your heel and walk quickly back to your room. You're so upset that your hands shake. You have to try twice to get the card to work in the door lock. You call 911 and explain the situation to the dispatcher. You say you are concerned for the boy and suggest they might want to send someone. You don't want to sound hysterical, or personally involved in any way. You don't give your name. Her tone makes it clear that she understands perfectly.

Your task done, you hang up and wonder what to do next. You don't want to be visible when the police arrive, or in the restaurant where the hotel staff might point you out—but you're hungry. You don't want to leave the hotel in search of another restaurant, just in case there might be a need for a dramatic, heroic rescue.

Uncertain as usual, you stand by your door peering out the peep hole, straining for sounds from the other room. It takes over ten minutes for the police to arrive. You time it.

A short, fat officer knocks smartly on their door. A taller cop stands just behind him and to the left. Then two more join them, eager for action. You can see them talking through the closed door, their bodies shortened and curved on the edges of your view, but you can't hear their words. Body language tells you the cops are getting annoyed. They start gripping various implements on their belts, and stand up straighter, looking stern and ready for trouble.

Finally the door opens and the officers flow in like an angry blue wave. Screaming starts again, and the woman shouts at the police to leave her alone. The door closes behind them, and then—nothing.

Silence.

Minutes pass until a flashing in the corner of your eye distracts you. You go to the window and see four police cars outside. A crowd has gathered. You feel a momentary sense of power, thinking about how they've come because of you. You stand a little straighter and half wish you had given your name so you could stride proudly outside and offer your report to the police and TV crews.

Why, you could've been famous.

You hear more noise in the hallway and decide the more interesting view might be through the peephole. You see a policewoman in the hallway with the little boy in her arms. His delicate little hand is stretched out toward the open hotel room door, and he's screaming, 'Momma,' over and over again. You notice bright red marks on his cheeks, no doubt where he was slapped.

Meanwhile, a woman you assume is Momma is being restrained by two large officers, with no great degree of gentleness. She stretches her hand out to the little boy, calling, 'Justin, my sweet little angel!'

The policewoman carries Momma's sweet little angel down the hall. When the boy is no longer in sight, the woman stops fighting and sags against the door frame. You examine her distorted face, expecting to see cruelty, savagery, a certain vulgar disdain for human life. It should be spelled out across her features, radiating from her eyes.

But you see no such thing. She looks worn, frightened and bone-weary. Her light brown hair is greying, and her soft face is beginning to sag. Her features seem faded.

The tall cop, who appears to be in charge, turns and starts to leave, but she lunges toward him, grabbing his arm. The other cops reach for their weapons, ready to gun her down. They're stopped right outside your door now, and the view is even better than you hoped.

'Where is he being taken? When will I get him back?'

'That's hard to say, ma'am. We'll have to see.'

'See? See what? I'm a good mother, I—'

'Yes, ma'am, I'm sure you are, but there were reports of abuse—'

'No! No, you don't understand. He just—the baby. I was running the bath for the baby, and Justin was trying to help. Don't you see?'

'Ma'am?'

'I just stepped away for a minute, just a minute to get my soda from the other room.'

'Yes, ma'am, I'm sure when the—'

'Justin must've thought he could help with the bath, but my baby nearly drowned when he put him in the bathtub and I—I just got so frightened.'

The officer nods reassuringly and tells her to explain it all to social services when they arrive. He then leads her back to the room as she starts to cry.

You hear her words and think it must be terrifying for her, poor woman, all alone with three kids in a hotel room. Where was her husband? Why didn't she have help?

But then your sympathy begins to fade. You wonder if it's true. She could have made the whole thing up. For a moment, you are ashamed of your thoughts. Or at least you feel you ought to be ashamed, but you have trouble working yourself up to it. What does any of it have to do with you? You did what you could to help.

You look through the peephole again. The hallway is empty, so you flip off the lights and leave your room, easing the door shut behind you. You step quickly, quietly down the hall toward the elevators. Although you can't help but hear the sobs coming from the woman's room, your steps don't falter. You ride the elevator down, walk outside to your car and set your sights on the neon lights down the road. You seek and find one of those comforting, convenient chain restaurants where the food is predictable and no one will demand anything of you but your order and, later, cash or a major credit card.

No personal checks, please.

Toxoplasme
Stefanie Dao

*S*TOP. *Take a deep breath. Let the air flow through your nostrils and into your lungs and out again over your tongue. What do you taste in the air? The warm, moist scent of earth, the sharp, itchy scent of pines, the sweet and delicate scents of endless varieties of flowers. But the earth and the flowers are of no interest to you. The scent you seek is not present.*

Keep moving. There is no living blood here. Move slowly, smoothly. Your body burns calories like fire through dry brush. Do not make unnecessary movements. Do not waste energy. Walk silently. Prey is skittish and will flee at the faintest sound. Do everything you must to gain the upper hand.

The sun scorches your head and neck. Burns, some from today, some acquired weeks ago, blister your skin.

You were the quiet one. She did all the talking, always smiling and speaking and laughing for both of you. She was brave and was never afraid to voice the things you were too unsettled to even think about. One of her late-night musings, drifting from a lofted bed across the stillness of a dormitory room, remains in your mind even to this day.

'We know so much about them, how they're made, what they eat. Every day we learn a new way to kill them. But why can't we figure out something as basic as whether or not they're still human inside?'

Pause. The forest looms darkly before you. Any blood scent is swallowed by the pungent odour of pine, but forests of this size and age mean that water is nearby. Water means life, and life means prey. Venture forward, every muscle taut and ready.

Lope silently into the shade. The sunlight is less intense than it was on the grassland. The trees catch the light as it falls, sprinkling and scattering it in speckled patterns that shift and dance with the wind across the forest floor. The ground is covered in dried needles that slice your feet. Your skin is deteriorating. You must eat soon or the degeneration will continue.

The terms they used were stark and sterile, as if their use would numb the horror. 'The brain,' they said, 'is the first organ to be affected. Within twenty hours, infected individuals will no longer respond to pain. Connections will start to form between the brain and the sensory organs, multiplying the individual's abilities exponentially.'

You wondered how it would feel to have a parasite hijack your brain and change it against your will. You wondered what else you might lose of yourself.

A professor showed two images on the projector. First, a healthy human, and then—invaded and ravaged by the parasite—an individual near death. He noted that the combined effects of increased metabolism and the parasite's rapid growth caused massive tissue atrophy and destruction at cellular level.

The slides made you want to vomit. Creatures reduced to skeletons, the disease had distorted their muscles and eaten away flesh and organs. Most had sores oozing on their skin and wounds that wouldn't heal, evidence of the parasite's suppression of all bodily functions except those required to move and eat. Many jaws were broken, unable to sustain the force their neck muscles delivered, so grotesquely bulked up due to the parasite's handiwork. You'd run a thumb along the edge of your own jaw and swallowed.

The river runs transparent and smooth like liquid glass. It smells of mud and decaying plant matter. No chemicals, medicines, or gasoline, poison it—the water is clean of human civilization. Yet there are no fish or frogs either. The river is dead.

Turn and follow the water upstream. As you make your way along the bank, the silence of the forest is all too obvious. No birds, no small animals, no predators lurking in the bush. The forest is dead as well.

Then, scent bursts upon you like a train out of the darkness. Your human nose would have called it sickening. Several smells mix: blood, flesh, decay, bacteria, and bear. The last scent is of no alarm. The bear is too cold, too still. Like the river and forest it is also dead. You are not surprised when you follow a bend in the river and see the mass, blackened and skeletal, stagnating half-in the water. It is dead and you cannot feed on it. Move on.

You'd sat there tracing your jawline, dreading what the professor would say next. Even though you knew it was coming, you were still shaken when he said it, using those same, sterile words. 'Infected individuals will inevitably expire. Neither vaccine nor treatment exists.'

In other words, once bitten, twice dead. Your thoughts on the matter haven't changed since then.

You don't want to die.

As you walk, taste the air again. Sort out the scent of the dead bear, as if untangling one thread from a ball of string. Discard it. Pick through what remains. There. Faint. Solid and wild and warm. Deer. The deer is alive.

Shift into hunting mode. Bend your knees, bring your centre of gravity closer to the ground. Hold out your arms for balance. Spread your toes and fingers, your overgrown nails turn into claws. Adrenaline primes your muscles and your breathing deepens, your lungs are like bellows feeding the fire in your stomach. You repress the urge to sprint—the prey is still far off, and your body still has its limits.

Smell it. The scent stands out like a glowing white line, leading you forward. The rest of the world disappears, a visual cacophony of rainbowed scents fading into grey. With long swift strides you make your way through the forest. You have not eaten in a week.

You see it through a screen of trees, standing, hesitating. Tan and brown, its whiffling black nose picks up the unfamiliar scent. It is unable to comprehend this thing that smells natural but unnatural, sweet and yet full of decay and blood.

Soon its blood will be yours, its tissue yours, because without it, you will die. A part of you, a tiny, timid fragment of your being, doesn't want to do this, but the rest of you roars out: you do not want to die!

See it. Do not be seen. Crouch. Hide. Breathe. Relax. You will have one chance. Strike and bring it down before your energy wanes.

The deer sees you out of one of its wide-set eyes, but before it can bolt you are on its back, claws digging into the thick hide, shredding it. Throw your head back for momentum, and then lunge forward. Your teeth and jaws could not be changed, but their power has been greatly amplified. Tear into its neck, through hair and hide, until you are suffocating in blood, drowning in the scent of hot metal. Your saliva flows, entering the wound. The deer's body spasms and collapses to the ground. Like a wolf you do not wait for it to die before feeding. The blood soaks your body. The meat twitches as you swallow it.

Finished with the slides, the professor moved on to the topic of transmission. 'The parasite is spread mainly through direct contact, particularly contact with infected blood and saliva. Transfer through air and water is also possible, so while you are in the field, do not remove the breathing apparatus until you are in an area known to be clean. The most immediate sign of infection is seizure, followed by paralysis.'

Afterwards, she was the only one who gave you any comfort. Something about her way of talking, her way of smiling, her way of laughing in the face of the hell that was around you, made you feel like things might turn out okay. One look in her eyes and you felt safe.

'Hey. You all right?'

'I—I'm fine,' you managed to say. You buried your face deeper into the pillow you clutched to your chest.

'I don't think you are.' The long, narrow bed creaked as she climbed up and sat next to you.

'Look,' she said, 'I know it's a lot to take in, but isn't this what we've been waiting for? Isn't this our chance? This is the time to take back our world.'

'Yeah. I guess.'

Quiet. Then she spoke, 'You know, I'm a little scared, too.'

You looked at her in surprise, forgetting to hide the tears on your face.

'I know,' she said, looking away as her cheeks turned red. 'Who wouldn't be? They're dangerous. You'd have to be an idiot not to be scared of them.'

You nodded. 'Yeah. It's just that—'

'What?'

A moment of hesitation.

'Do you really think they're still human? Deep down, somewhere?' A long silence. She stared at you. Incredulous at first, then sympathetic.

'You miss them, don't you?'

While you cried, she laid an arm around your shoulders. It was warm, solid, alive, safe.

'I think,' she said softly, 'that if they are still in there, they'll understand. Because there are people who are still alive, who want to keep on living, and it's our job to protect them. We've tried for years to find a cure and there's nothing, so this is all we can do. It's brutal and despicable and disgusting, but we have to. If they're still in there, I think they'll understand. They'll forgive you.'

You don't notice the trap until it is upon you. From beneath the fragrant needles, from beneath the treacherous earth, it leaps, snapping you up in a mess of dirt and deer and blood. It has solid walls and a ceiling of wires. The wire is strong. Slash at it, bite at it until your fingers and gums are torn. It was bait. The deer was bait. There is a Hunter nearby.

You howl, claw, and batter your body against the wire. You are the predator, not the prey. You will kill whoever did this. Footsteps approach. Somebody is coming. You will kill whoever did this to you.

A helmet appears on the other side of the wire mesh. Human eyes stare at you through a yellow-tinted visor. Claw, snap, roar. You do not care who it is. You will kill them.

The muzzle of a gun sits at point-blank range. You have no room to manoeuvre. The gun is shaking. The human is shaking. Her finger is on the trigger, but she does not pull it. It is because she is weak. She is weak, and you are strong. Slam your body against the wires, against the walls. The walls are weak. They will fall. She will fall next.

Nobody could have prevented the accident. The trap malfunctioned and the parasite got in through a thin spot in your armour, near your left elbow joint. You knew they had to shoot you. But you didn't want to die.

You dove into the river, pulsating waves of pain driving you mad. The rapids and rocks battered your armour and tore it to pieces, but the breathing apparatus continued to function. The current carried you downriver until finally it deposited you on a sandy shore where you rose from the shattered wreck that had been the sign of your cadet-level Hunter status. You staggered on, away from the shouts of your teammates, away from their guns, away from the death that would have taken you then.

The wires are giving. Throw your entire weight against them. Your skin is torn and blood coats the metal, but the wires are bending.

The human stands there—she stands there—silent, still, holding her gun, but not pulling the trigger. What is she waiting for? End this, shoot! Do it!

A wire snaps. That is all you need. You burst through the top of the cage, free. The wires shred your torso as you pull away from the wreckage, but the only thing on your mind is the human, and that you will kill her.

She jumps back as you escape your prison. She is afraid but catches herself and raises the gun. You lunge. Your muscles are tense. Your joints, locked. Your heart beats so fast it hums. Escape! You are strong enough, fast enough. You are still alive.

But then your body stops. You don't feel anything. And in that brief, final moment, the last part of you that is still you forgives her.

BLOOD SONG
Alexis A Hunter

EMPTINESS grows inside your chest, a void that screams in silence. There's a fire in her smile and two round scars on the side of her ivory neck. Her lips part as she moves. Hips swaying, she traces an invisible ribbon that connects her to you. Your heart aches as she approaches. Your gut twists and your lungs burn. She teaches you to feel alive, although she herself is dead.

You hear music in the silence. Your blood a fluttering tempo. Your heart pounding out the bass. She reaches you and you can't breathe. She falls upon you. You tremble, spellbound, as she places her lips in the curve of your neck. Her fangs break through, a splash of warmth. Teeth probe swollen veins and explode lacing capillaries. The music fades as darkness sweeps in.

'Thank you,' you gasp with the last of your breath. She holds you as this song reaches its decrescendo and the final, weakening beats sound. In that moment, she is yours—and you, hers.

Desire sated. Peace secured.

Set free by the demon, you'll sing her praises in the netherworld.

You Weren't Heavy
Laura Dunkeyson

You weren't heavy. I carried you over the ice and up the steps. You seemed tired and we'd only walked from the car. You were slipping on the frosty bits of the path, I didn't think you'd be able to cope on the ice and I didn't want you to fall, and once I was carrying you it just seemed easier to continue up the steps.

When I picked you up I could feel your bones, even with two jumpers and my spare coat on. It was as if they were hollow. You told me once that bird's bones were hollow. Back when the cat used to leave them on the rug in the living room and I used to give them a funeral and bury them in the garden. I'd hold them so gently, balanced in the palm of my hand. It felt like I would crush them if I held them any other way. You felt like that when I picked you up, like you were a bird. You started to fuss around when we got inside. You wanted to open the windows and air the house, to show me to the spare room, to check the use by dates in the fridge, but after only one step your legs quivered and you faltered.

'Why don't I make a cup of tea?' I said, too loudly, too brightly. You nodded and laughed that laugh you used to save for teachers and the vicar's wife. We were still feeling it out, what we could talk about, what was off limits, what our new roles were.

Your kitchen was organised logically and I had no trouble finding the tea bags in the cupboard above the kettle. They were in the little tin with the William Morris print. It was rusting around the dent in the side, the one from when I dropped it all those years ago. I made the tea in the teapot. I wouldn't usually have bothered but you always said it didn't taste right if it was made in the mug. When I took the tea through to the living room, you were settled into the armchair by the fireplace. You smiled at me and I knew I was forgiven for carrying you.

We were quiet while we drank the tea. I didn't know what to say. I wanted to know what you were thinking about, if you were thinking about all this, about what was happening. I didn't want to ask. Your hand was shaking each time you lifted the mug to your mouth. I wanted to ask you if you were OK, but instead I got up to put the gas fire on.

'You've got to waggle the knob a little,' you said, before I'd even started to struggle. Later, while you were lying down I wandered back into the living room. I stood in the doorway, eyes closed, and breathed deeply. Freesias and lavender: your perfume. Then leather, polish, and something else. Something sweet and hot yet also slightly sour. The smell of sickness, of bleached bones: earthy but powdery. When I opened my eyes and looked around the room I couldn't help but smile. Against the back wall, facing the fireplace, the old sofa welcomed me in. You'd had it cleaned. The fingertip marks were gone from the arms, and the tear on the left side was neatly sewn up. The patchwork cushions we'd made nestled into the seat. A low bookcase in the corner housed your travel guides, fifty plus volumes, creases down their spines, corners turned and worn. At the end of the shelf was our atlas. I loved that atlas. Lying on our stomachs on the floor we closed our eyes and travelled all over the world. Picking out places for you to read about, your voice painting warm breezes, crashing waves, and frying spices.

A crowd of faces smiled out at me from the mantelpiece. You had photos of everything—our first days at school, Sarah's graduation, me in the school play. There were summer holidays with posed shots in front of the caravan and next to sandcastles on empty windswept beaches. Grandma and Grandpa were standing outside their front door, under the rose arbour, waving and smiling. There was Sarah and Mark's wedding day, with me in the lemon bridesmaid dress. And so many baby pictures of Brandon and Findlay. Where is Sarah now, though? That's what I wanted to ask. Surely nothing in anyone's life should have been more important than being with you then. Next to the wedding photos was the snapshot of me and Jeff that I'd sent to you. It was taken in Berlin last year. I was squinting crookedly into the camera and he had his usual perfect smile. I was considering replacing it with a different photo when I heard you calling from upstairs.

You were still in bed when I got there. I marvelled at how nice you'd made the room. It was bright and airy, all blues and creams. Your dreams marched across the walls, contained within frames. Sweeping beaches, forested valleys, brightly painted cafés. My eyes lingered over them and I could almost taste the clean, new air. My ticket to these dreams, one-way to a new world, was safely tucked away in my bag. But it seemed as unreal now as the dreams of childhood. I wanted to tell you. I nearly did. But in the late afternoon sun that streamed through the windows and fell across the bed, you seemed so small. You barely made a dint in the pillow. You said the light was hurting your head and asked me to pull the curtains. You said you just wanted to sleep a little more. I asked you about dinner but you were noncommittal. You didn't get up again that day. You didn't want the soup I brought to you. You were tired, so very tired. I left you to sleep and sat downstairs, worrying.

The next day you seemed better, brighter and a little stronger. But I had spoken to the doctor before we left the hospital so I knew. You came downstairs and we had breakfast in the kitchen, overlooking the garden. You fretted about the birds not having been fed while you were away and I poured mounds of seed onto the bird table. They flocked down, swooping and diving for the feed, like they had been waiting the whole time. I had to put a second lot out for them, because you were worried about the more timid ones, the wagtails and blue tits that were chased away by the cheeky, aggressive robins. That was so like you. You told me about the different birds that came and how you even had a jay there last summer. You told me about your garden and what you had grown this year. You told me what you were planning to plant in the spring. I offered to help you dig it over.

We got into a routine over those few weeks. Every morning I took you a cup of tea and set out the pills for the day on the bedside table. You tried to hide it but I could tell from those few minutes how the day was going to be, how bad the pain would be, how clear your mind would be. There was no pattern to which days were good and which were bad. I knew you found this frustrating.

I sat at the foot of the bed sipping my tea while you took your pills. I'd felt you looking at me, and when I turned around, your eyes narrowed, like they always did when you were thinking.

'How's Jeff?' you asked.

'Fine.' I'm sure he was. 'He's always fine.' I decided not to mention that the girl in the café would be a better person to ask than me. Your eyes were still narrowed though, and you pursed your lips slightly.

'I was thinking that a late-summer wedding would be nice.'

'Hmmm?'

'How about September?' You were watching me intently. 'I can help you plan it, like I did for Sarah.'

'I'd like that.' And believe me, there was nothing I would have liked more.

You smiled, satisfied. I twisted the ring around my finger, thankful I hadn't been able to bring myself to take it off yet. I really am sorry I didn't tell you. I just didn't want to upset you; I thought it might be bad for you. I told myself I'd tell you when you started to improve. But, buried at the back of my head, the thought that it may never matter just wouldn't go away.

On a Wednesday, a good day, you asked me to help sort through some things. *So I wouldn't have to go through all that old stuff later.* This first acknowledgement took me aback. I hauled boxes filled with old magazines, winter coats, and jam jars down from the loft, climbing one-handed up and down the rickety ladder. You carried a box downstairs but the effort exhausted you and you sat trembling in the chair. We sorted through old records: Joni Mitchell, Joan Baez, Bob Dylan. It was the music that was playing each day when I charged home from school, to you, waiting with juice and a sliced apple. The house even smelt of your coffee again. We moved from the loft to the hall cupboard where shelves of shoes gathered dust—old boots with still supple leather, twenty-year-old high heels, sandals with remnants of sand worn into the seams. A box right at the back, behind a broken but mendable vacuum cleaner, held my ballet shoes. The metallic scent of blood lingered in the pointes.

Finally, we reached the chest in the corner of the living room. Packed to the top, it revealed winters of matching woollen dresses and brightly patterned wellies. Summers of garden-digging and holidays in Scarborough when—still wearing our identical dresses—Sarah and I charged into the sea, eager to be in those foamy waves.

You turned a photo over in your hands, straightened out a folded corner and read the note on the back, *North Bay Sands, Summer 1986.* You passed me the photo.

'Do you remember that summer?' Captured by the camera, Sarah and I victoriously waved streamers of seaweed. Off to the left, looking into the distance as if already gone, a man in red shorts. It took me a moment to recognise him; it had been so long since I'd seen a picture.

'I remember the seaweed. We spent hours collecting it.' I was reluctant to mention him. 'Then Sarah snatched mine and chased me with it.'

You frowned, 'I'm sure she wouldn't do that.'

I snorted slightly. 'When she caught me she shoved the whole lot down my back.' The smell never completely washed out of the dress. It had been my favourite. My nose wrinkled again at the thought.

'She always looked after you.'

'Hmmm.'

'You used to sit outside the caravan sharing the things you'd collected that day, just junk—pebbles, shells, and stuff. She always made sure you had more than her. She used to help you find somewhere safe to store it. You used to call it sea treasure.'

I don't remember this at all. It doesn't fit with my memories of Sarah as an older sister. I was going to say this but then you started smiling. Your eyes were unfocused. I guess you were seeing two little girls filled with holiday joy. Abruptly you looked back at me.

'Don't be too harsh on her, she was older, she remembered more.' You looked at the photo again and I knew you were looking at him. Your hand hesitated, a finger almost reaching out to touch the figure. 'That was the last summer.'

I didn't have anything to say.

We dug deeper into the chest, casting ghosts across the living room. End of year projects from school, Christmas cards, Easter nests, a lumpy clay ashtray painted with flowers, all lurked among the folds of a crocheted baby blanket. Then, hidden under the older mementos, there were folders of papers and travel brochures. I started to pull them out but your slight gasp and widened eyes stopped me.

'I'm tired,' you protested quietly. 'We've done lots today.' You were watching me, waiting for a reaction. But I didn't know how to react. 'Let's have a cup of tea and one of those nice cakes you bought.'

Those nice cakes you'd turned your nose up at yesterday. I played along though, I let myself be distracted but I knew what lay at the bottom of the chest. I was old enough to remember the promise of a new world, and the happy evenings spent pouring over brochures and pictures. You danced with us, just as excited, as we read about hot, sunny Christmases, landscapes covered with trees and cities full of opportunities. How could I not remember? We looked at houses, schools, jobs, and plotted our escape. Year after year the brochures re-emerged, but each time they would eventually disappear, and a bit more of you would go with them. Later, when you were sleeping, I looked through the papers. Emigration forms, residency papers, passport applications, all empty, waiting. Why had we never left? Why had we never made the dream come true? I never asked you. I told myself the time never felt right, but I didn't want to know. I didn't want to hear about regrets and lost dreams, to realise your cowardice when it was too late. But here it all was, too much of a temptation. Here were pages of carefully kept accounts. Years of household expenditure, catalogued. Each month's money carefully put aside, gradually building, reaching out to the new world. Only to be sucked away by school uniforms, birthday parties and ballet lessons.

As I turned each page the cost of our childhood stared out at me. Here, a smashed window from next-door's conservatory. I felt your anger anew, first with me, then directed at Mr Richards when he called me a little hooligan and blamed your lack of control. Here, another destroyed bike, crashed racing down the hill, one dare too many. Here, compensation paid to local shops to drop the charges, stolen lipsticks and earrings once cheap, now cripplingly expensive.

The price of childhood innocence pulled the papers from my hands. You never said. You never even hinted. I sank onto the carpet, unable to move. But then a hope flickered. Maybe it wasn't too late, maybe I could take you with me. We could go together, start a new life, rebuild the years that have passed in silence and distance. But when I reached your doorway another dream faded. Your skin was mushroom-like under my touch. I tried to stroke away the pain, but it was etched too deeply into your face, a permanent twist to your mouth, indelible lines round your eyes, and all I could do was sit with silent sobs shaking my chest. My ticket, my escape, cowered in my bag, mocking, as you slipped further away and the house fell into darkness around me.

When the end was coming I called the rest of them—Sarah and Mark and their boys, Uncle Phillip and Aunt Mary. They all gathered round your bedside. Your eyes lit up as they arrived, pressing your hand between theirs. Speaking through a thick haze, you said hello, telling off their damp cheeks and catching voices. I was just relieved to hear you speak. I sat in the corner, on the old rocking chair, and watched. I thought I was ready. Your hair was fanned out across the pillow like fading, thinning sunshine. You'd always been so proud of your hair; at least it hadn't fallen out, the disease too advanced for that treatment. I ran my fingers along the edge of the ticket in my pocket. I hadn't had to change the date after all. You hadn't lasted to know of my escape. The paper slipped and sliced. I looked at the oozing blood and tasted earth and metal on my tongue. You were dissolving round the edges, blending into the pillow. I watched quietly from the corner as you finally faded away. You had made me promise I wouldn't cry; you told me my eyes looked so much prettier when they weren't puffy and red, but I couldn't, and silent tears ran down my cheeks as I called the doctor in.

Last Funeral But Two
E A M Harris

As the postman handed me the parcel, I thought of you, Amy. Who else would send me something so heavy and at least a foot square, wrapped in brown paper and parcel tape?

Now I'm sitting at the kitchen table, looking at it, eating my breakfast and thinking of you. I'd like to say my thoughts are warm and cosy. Some are, but they are mixed with cold, worrywart ones. I think about how, after the funeral, you gave me a lift.

I felt all bubbly inside with gratitude and when you offered to help sort our cousin Muriel's house, the bubbles got bigger. Her landlord, who'd let Muriel take over her parents' lease, deserved to get his bungalow back quickly. Not that he'd said anything, except for condolences, but Muey would've wanted him considered—she was always grateful to him.

'Oh, thank you, Amy. That would be marvellous.' I'm not one for words like marvellous, but I thought you might need encouraging. I didn't know you well enough to tell—still don't. We would have grown up together and really known each other, but you and your mother moved away. After that, we only met at funerals. And if there's one good thing about a departure, it's that you can strengthen old acquaintances.

As we bounced between the gravestones towards the cemetery exit in your four-wheel drive, I pictured Muey flying above us. From up there she could overlook all of Croydon and beyond—particularly at this time of year with the trees still bare. She would see the office blocks where people came from all over, even London, to work. She'd see the twisty roads and cul-de-sacs of the new estates, and the older parts, following high streets and old village greens, where Muey and I and almost everyone we knew have always lived. I imagined her watching the two of us as we rode together.

We air-kissed goodbye.

You said, 'I'll be there at eight tomorrow.'

'That's earlier than I can get there. I haven't got a car, and I must see to my neighbour's cat, and—'

'No problem. Give me a key and I'll start by myself.'

'I can't do that. There's only one.'

'My dear Shirley, I'll give it back as soon as you come.'

'I know, but if something happens overnight it's me who'll get called.'

'What could happen? Are there valuables someone might steal?'

'I doubt it. She—'

'Don't you know? I thought you used to go and look after her. People like her are generally very poor, so I've heard.'

I clambered out of your car.

You waved, 'I'll get there at nine then. Will you be there? I don't want to stand on the doorstep.'

At first, everything went as I hoped. You told me about your job in the library and listened when I told you about mine—not so different really—in hospital records. But Muey was the reason we were together, and it was only respectful to talk about her sometimes. Like when you picked up her blue, cut-glass vase.

'I remember that,' I said. 'Muey bought it from a scruffy boy who came to the door. I'm sure it was stolen, but she said it was cheap and that he looked honest. She was such a softy.'

You just shrugged and put the vase down on the kitchen windowsill. The sun, shining through the window, sent fingers of blue light splaying across the white tiles. I thought of a ghost clinging to its old home.

The only time you offered an opinion, we were standing shoulder to shoulder, looking at the painting of a country church.

'I remember that picture. It was here when Rachel and Ed were alive and we all used to play here. It's ghastly. I'm amazed Muriel kept it.'

'Auntie Rachel painted it,' I said.

'Really? Well I suppose that's a reason for her hanging on to it. You're not going to keep it, are you?'

'No, I haven't room for it and I've already got several of her paintings. It can go to the Hospice shop.'

You sighed. 'Why not the RSPCA, it's nearer?'

'They've already had two loads and Muey would want some things to go to the Hospice. She was in there, you know—no I suppose you don't—but she was there until she came home near the very end. She would want them to benefit; she was always grateful to them.'

Muey wasn't a hoarder. Sometimes I arrived at her house to find a black sack in the hall and she'd ask me to take it to the charity shop. We'd discuss which one. She spread her donations around. I think it made her feel she was giving more.

'My dear Shirley,' you said as you lifted sacks into the back of your car, 'the RSPCA is much nearer and parking is so much easier.'

I helped you. You're as short as I am and the sacks were heavy.

'It's what Muey would've wanted.' Usually I'm not one to press an issue.

'Whatever.' You climbed into the driver's seat. 'I'll see you tomorrow.'

Credit to you though; you made a fuss, but I saw that picture in the Hospice shop a few days later.

The next day we started in the living room. I tugged open the thick curtains. It was a real March day outside. The light that came in was streaming and waving as it coiled through the bare branches of the bushes in the front garden. It flickered across the carpet until it arrived at the coffee table in front of the fireplace. There, it caught the photo frames and the gilt clock, making them look as if they were reflecting fire. I felt a lump in my throat, remembering how often it had done that.

You walked over to the table, bent down and picked up the clock. I was about to tell you that she'd bought it from Woolworth's, on a March day just like today, when you took a little book out of your pocket. I looked over your shoulder. *Collectibles and their Value Today*, it was called.

You flicked past pictures of all sorts of things. The prices were staggering. Another word I don't often use, but £1,000 for a jug which wouldn't hold a pint!

The clock wasn't there.

I tried to tell you some things about Muey—little memories that make up a person that I wanted someone else to know, but you went on folding curtains and said nothing, so I stopped. *We're the last of our family*, I thought, *when my time comes, no one will know. It'll be like she never even existed*. I suppose I should have done something about it, but

I couldn't decide what.

You worked quickly, and sorted and cleaned as if born to it—which you were I suppose, your mother having been Uncle Brian's charlady before she married him.

We left Muey's bedroom until last. It had been her room all her life and was the most cluttered. Seventy-two years leave a trail no matter how much you clear out.

Late in the afternoon, we took the black sacks and Hoover and started. I'd opened the window earlier so there was a nip in the room, but the smell of emptiness had gone.

The bed was already stripped.

'This is where she was when she was called,' I said.

'Don't tell me that, Shirley. I can guess it for myself. I don't want to talk about it.'

So we worked without talking. I was kind of glad you were there, and kind of not. If you hadn't been there I would've worked more slowly and lingered over her things. But I would've felt sadder, and even though it annoyed me when you dropped her diaries into the sacks as if touching them might hurt, and looked in your little book when you opened the Tupperware box where she kept her few jewels, I was less sad with you there.

Then we opened the wardrobe.

Muey had been proud of that wardrobe. It was the built-in kind, the length of a whole wall. She'd paid one of her neighbours to build it when he was out of work.

'Good God,' you said. 'What on earth are these doing here?'

I was standing behind you so couldn't see what you meant.

'Look at this lot.' You bent down and picked something up off the wardrobe floor, then turned to me. In each hand you held a pair of shoes, wrapped in clear plastic like giant sandwich bags. They were dusty, but not very; Muey must have dusted them shortly before she fell ill. The shoes were new.

Looking at them, I sat down on the bed. I could feel the tears coming. I'd held them back all the time we'd been together, but now I couldn't.

I opened one of the bags and shook the shoes out. They were the colour we used to call gunmetal grey, with chisel toes and stiletto heels.

I can remember shoes like that coming out more than thirty years ago.

You were fiddling in the wardrobe again.

'Look at all this!' You had armfuls. You spread them over the bed.

'Look at these!' You pulled out a pair of dancing shoes, tearing the bag as you did. They were black slingbacks, covered in sequins and little feathers. They were beautiful. They made me sob.

'It's pathetic,' you said, putting the shoes down.

I wanted to protest but I was crying too hard, so I just shook my head.

'Yes it is, Shirley. God, talk about wishful bloody thinking.' You tore the bag off a pair of knee-length boots with high heels like girls wear with trousers.

I shook my head again and glanced at Muey's wheelchair. The shoes she'd really worn were on the foot-rest. We'd been walking round it ever since we started the room. It was so much a part of her that I hadn't had the heart to move it out.

'People should face things,' you said as you put more pairs on the bed. 'There's no point weeping about it. She knew she was just a cripple.'

'You shouldn't say *just* or *cripple*, that's not right,' I sounded so choked I don't think you understood me. You didn't answer. Then you started lining up the shoes; I couldn't think what you were up to. You smiled.

'Do you realise that some of these date from just after the war? Look at these. I saw them once in a costume display. She must have bought a new pair every two or three years.' You picked up a pair of pink sandals. You looked serious. 'Is it pathetic, though? After all, it is a real collection. They're all new. There are collectors who would pay real money for these. We must see an auctioneer or something.'

I expected you to read your book again, but you seemed to have decided the shoes were valuable anyway.

You've no right to call Muey pathetic or question what she did. I didn't want to start a quarrel—not there in her room. It wasn't respectful. I stood up.

'We've got to finish this room,' I said. 'It's late and I promised to feed the cat again. Leave them and we'll go on.'

You agreed, thank goodness, but you kept going on about who to call to find out what the shoes were worth. I didn't bother answering.

'I'll phone up a couple of auctioneers in the morning,' you told me as you got into the car. 'I'll see you about lunch time.'

Most of the night I sat wondering what to do with the shoes, trying to work out what Muey would have wanted.

Carrying them to the disabled children's shop was difficult on the bus. I'd bagged them so there was enough sack for me to grip, but I had to make two journeys. It was worth it. When I told the manageress that as a collection they may be valuable, she excitedly told me that one of her volunteers knew about such things.

I think they'll get more money than you. Collectors would have beaten your price down, but they'll be more generous to children.

You were furious.

'How could you give them away? They were the only things in the house worth anything. I think you should have considered me, after all the help I've given you.'

'I'm sorry to upset you. You can take anything you want of what's left, even the things I've put aside for myself.'

After being up most of the night I was too tired to argue. Besides, I didn't want to completely lose my last relation.

What you said then made me go all cold. 'My dear Shirley, have you thought of why Muriel created that collection? You don't understand collecting, but I do. So, apparently, did Muriel. She must have worked hard to build that up. Now you've sent her work away. Her collection will be broken up or sold to a foreigner.'

I tried to imagine Muey as a collector. I asked myself if you could be right. All those shoes, and the thought that there was something so big about Muey that I hadn't known, had really thrown me. I tried to tell myself that I'd done the right thing, but the words wouldn't come.

I feel awful now, sitting at the kitchen table, looking at the parcel. We didn't exactly part friends, though we did have a cup of tea together. Only the future will show if strengthening an old acquaintance worked this time. I've tried not to think about it all—you, the shoes, Muey being a collector—but every time I walk past the disabled children's shop it comes back, and I feel terrible. Have I really destroyed her life's work?

I get the scissors and cut the parcel's paper. It's not from you!

Inside is a box with a letter from Muey's landlord. He writes kindly, hoping I'm well and saying he misses Muey as a tenant.

His letter ends:

> *I found these in the house. They must have slipped off the wheelchair step when you moved it. I hope you don't mind me sending them to you, but I didn't know what to do with them.*

I open the box. Inside are Muey's real shoes. They're big, stretched to fit her swollen feet. Both soles are built up so she could reach the wheelchair footrest, but one of them is much thicker than the other. I go all cold again, but then I pick up the heavy shoes.

Then the cold rushes away. I know I've done the right thing.

THE END OF THE LINE
Cathryn Grant

I didn't mean to bloody your lip. The situation escalated too quickly. But that's putting it nicely because I'm feeling like a thug for splitting your pale flesh with a thin crevice that spouted an unbelievable amount of bright red liquid. You were pushy, one of those types who thinks the rules don't apply to you. What you didn't know is that I'm one of those other types, compelled to enforce the rules.

My husband and I arrived early because we know how quickly the line grows at Stella's Crab and Chowder house and that morning—as the sun crested the foothills and sparkled on the Pacific Ocean—we were sure the outside seating would be snapped up fast. The corner table sits apart, a private oasis with a view of the harbour and the entire span of the bay. We call ourselves creatures of habit, and we are. We like the front table on the patio and are willing to loiter outside the locked doors, wasting thirty minutes of a glorious day, just to get that table.

But then you came scurrying up and wriggled between my husband's elbow and the cart displaying items from the gift shop. You scooted past him up to the door. You grabbed the handle and pulled. In that quick scuttle and tug I knew what kind of person you were—either so arrogant you thought you could circumnavigate your way around what's right, or too stupid to recognize that the line of ten people meant the restaurant wasn't open. Did you think we were in line because it never occurred to us to try opening the door?

No one else seemed bothered. Or maybe they were all watching you as warily as I was, although I pretended to keep my eyes demurely on my 600–page, hardbound book. One page took me fifteen minutes to digest as I watched you fuss and wriggle and dance around, hoping it wasn't really a line. You were certain that when the door opened you'd be right there in front. You'd dart inside and the staff and patrons would be too polite to grab your gold and burgundy silk scarf and yank you back where you belonged—at the end of the line.

You disappeared and returned. Twice. Repeatedly pressing your face against the glass, peering inside, as if servers readying themselves for a non-stop flood of sun seekers wanted to yield their last moments of tranquillity to you.

The manager bent down, inserted his key into the lock and pulled the door wide, his smile equally open, eager to invite his guests inside.

Despite my icy glare, despite our solid position at the front of the line, you actually pushed against me as you went through the open door.

I walked in as calmly as I could. I know I was calm because my husband said, somewhat louder than necessary, *Calm down.* He knows me.

You marched forward, your chin jutting up, and your scarf flowing behind you like spilled wine down the back of your white blouse.

I moved closer. The hostess looked up at you and asked how many were in your party. As smoothly as if I'd rehearsed it—and maybe I had—I closed my book, swung it up as if to put it into my oversized bag, and let my arm move toward your face as you continued to move toward the hostess stand. The sound of the book on your skin and teeth was not loud, but the force stopped you in your tracks.

I apologized profusely. *I'm so clumsy, so sorry. What a terrible accident*, smiling and lifting my long blonde hair over my shoulder. I looked down at my toes, covered in buttery leather boots, and let a blush bloom across my cheeks. Blonde hair is something that makes people look on me with affection, forgiving what they might not in others. But the air was like paper-thin crystal, everyone taking shallow breaths, convinced I'd very much intended to smack your face with the book.

The hostess pulled sheets of tissue out of a box under the counter and pressed them to your lip. The white instantly turned red. As she handed you more, the manager intervened.

'Let's get people seated,' he said.

We stated our preference for outside seating and followed a young girl out the door, down the steps, and across the empty patio to our waiting table.

Minutes later, you were seated at the table a few feet from ours. I turned to face the ocean, annoyed by my bad luck.

The server paused at our table to drop off her plans. *I'll be right back. I need to check whether that poor lady needs ice. If she doesn't do* something soon, her lip will be as big as her chin.'

It took forever. She returned with ice carefully wrapped in a towel, and a bottle of wine and a chiller. She uncorked the bottle and poured white wine into the four glasses on your table. The wine glistened in the sunlight.

She approached my left elbow, blocking my view of the bay. 'Can I start you with some drinks?'

My husband ordered the priciest bottle of Chardonnay on the menu. It would be the perfect complement to fresh crab, at the peak of its season.

'I'm sorry,' said the server. 'We only stock a few bottles of that one. The table behind you just ordered the last one.'

You couldn't have known. I recognize that, but still I felt you grinning behind my back, your split lip pulled taut until fresh blood seeped from the wound.

THE ILLUMINATED BACK
Nina Milton

SKIN is the story of our life. From the moment we hit air and bawl, it absorbs everything. New love, new hope, shattered dreams, burning hate. The rooms we pass through, the landscapes we breathe, the touch of each person we meet. No wonder our skin starts out so soft and full of moisture, then dries up as the years pass, until it is as flaky as an old pasty, and as thin as silk, barely covering the blood vessels below.

I wanted so much to be an aromatherapist. I was fed up of calling myself bar assistant, shop assistant, care assistant. I was fed up of being asked for non-existent GCSEs in maths and English. The only certificate I had was my *decree nisi*. But after the holistic massage course, I had diplomas hanging on the walls all round my room. I had clients who made appointments, respected my opinion, came back for more. Sometimes I put my cheek against the towels, just to feel their spongy whiteness and take in the faint aroma of scented oils.

I didn't want to give up this job, but the touch of skin was wearing me down. I wasn't sleeping and when I did I dreamt of layers...prickle, granular, clear and horn.

For a man of thirty-six, Jordon Brown had weathered skin. His hair was a razor-cut and he wore fatigue trousers with pockets covering every centimetre. Small pockets on top of larger pockets. A chain running from the belt to a pocket. The belt was a Doberman's collar. He sat on the client's chair with his legs splayed, trouser hems ruckled into boots that would've kept him stable on the moon.

I asked if there were any underlying conditions I should know about. Diabetes? Heart problems? Daft questions. You couldn't wear those boots if your heart was weak.

'I'm fit,' he said. 'I just fancied a massage.'

'Good. I'll be using some strongly scented oils. Is that okay?' Butch smells, I was hinting. He dipped his chin—a monosyllabic nod.

'Perhaps you'd like to get undressed and pop onto the couch?' He was out of his zipped and belted trousers in seconds. 'Just lie on your tummy and stay warm under the towels.'

I flipped the play button and the faint echoes of a harp's circular tune floated across the room. I blended cedar with bergamot and a little frankincense, oils that would help those fit muscles relax. I used grapeseed as a carrier. It's lighter, and I like a lot of slip when I massage. I blended the oils by shaking them in a clean blue glass bottle. I warmed them by standing the bottle in a little tub of hot water.

I peeled the towel from Jordon's back.

When I started out, I didn't get the anticipatory sensations. The words and pictures came to me after I'd been running my hands through the softness of a person's skin for some time. But lately, it's got so I only have to look at a back to shudder. The back is the largest area of skin the masseuse can examine that does not curve or curl but is simply a flat landscape. Mostly, the landscape is plain, pink or tan or Africa black. I expected Jordon's landscape to be as weathered as his face. I expected the usual whispers of anticipation, the responsive quivers from my own skin.

But Jordon was illuminated. Tattoos swirled and crocheted over him until no skin was left unmarked or uncoloured. I could not speak or move as I took in the surface story. A creature's face: feathers, teeth, tongue and the raw redness of an enraged throat, and inside that, patterns and letters furled out like a banner. *Rise above.*

As if advising me—you must rise above this. My hand shook badly. The little pool of blended oil in the centre of my palm had a surface tremor.

In diploma class we had to learn the benefits, origins and contraindications of the essential oils. We learnt to isolate their scents. We had to know composition of the skin, the name and position of the muscles, the effects of massage on internal structures, and formulas of touch—the way the hands stroke or knead the skin. A lot for me to take in, care assistant, shop assistant. Some things came easier than others.

The oils were a pushover. Their smells intrigued me. Bergamot was the smell of Auntie Joyce's tea. Cypress was the short-cut through the pine plantation. It was easy to pick out ginger, mint, tea tree or lavender, but soon I could discern between rose and geranium, marjoram and thyme, orange and mandarin. The oils sorted something in my head. I could smell how healing they were.

I learnt the muscles like a horror movie. The pictures in the text books leered out at me; humans flayed of their skin presenting the muscles that lie beneath, their eyes as haunting as the dead. Muscles take Latin titles—biceps, triceps, quadriceps, pectorals, rectus abdominus—but shorten them and you prevent the tongue muscle getting tied in knots. Bi's, tri's, quads, pecs, abs. I marched through the muscles and got an A.

Learning skin was a problem. There were too many layers, with names like a poem—*stratum germinativum, stratum spinosum, stratum granulosum, stratum lucidum, stratum corneum, papillary and reticular.* And the cells were worse—melanocyte for pigmentations; Langerhan, the immune system and Merkel cells, which are a mystery.

I gave them nicknames—basal, prickle, granular, clear and horn, butterfly and spider, Mel, Lang and Mystery Merk—I liked the idea of mystery because I couldn't visualize the layers of the skin. Their fineness confused me, the way they shifted, constantly rubbing themselves from existence as new layers moved up a layer ladder. I stared at pictures of cut-away skin, hairs growing out and fine wormholes carrying sweat and oil from the depths to the surface, and then at my own skin, which bore no resemblance. It was thin, so *pinchable*, but also so huge, so *ubiquitous*.

Then I put my hands on my first client, and I understood how this body covering sees all, experiences everything.

Jordon Brown was fit, all right. Pecs were a stage show. Tri's and bi's played a tune. Quads as taut as guy ropes, abs like iron. But the skin of his back, every pore, every hair, was covered by his tattoo. *Rise above.*

I had to start. He was lying there with his multicoloured back exposed above the shock of white towel. I laid my hands at the base of his spine. My stomach turned over. I dug the heel of my hand deep into those muscles, over the roaring beast and the banner's furl. I braced my body. This skin did not murmur at me. It screamed.

I'm in a place of sand. The ground is sand. The high walls are bricks of sand. The men have faces of sand and clothes the colour of wet sand. Our backs are against the wall, tight to its solidity. A line of hardened warriors.

The man in front turns. Flicks his fingers. No words. The hands speak. An infantryman runs forward, head down. The weapon across his back is long, black. He puts the toe of his boot against the irregularities of the wall and shins up it, with some help from a colleague's shoulder. He's our best.

Recon. A shitty job, to shin up the wall and peer over it. If a bullet takes your face, you have no chance. When he drops down, he is layered in sweat, but smiling. Good news. Good recon. He pushes back his helmet and rubs his forehead.

It is Jordon.

I was still learning to identify the various massage strokes when I realized my hands were super-sensitive. Effleurage, the gentlest stroke. Petrissage, where the fingers lift, roll and squeeze the skin. Kneading, which loosens the knots and adhesions in the muscles. Friction, which builds up warmth over a circular area. Tapping, hacking, and using pressure over the points of the meridians which in Chinese tradition are the healing channels of your body. And the gentlest stroke of all, to finish, a tickling of the fingers down the back, to leave your client with a sensation of total, accepting, love.

We massaged each other, us students, learning the strokes, giving feedback. A voice would float up from the hole in the couch. *Yeah, great, especially that last bit.* So, at first, I hardly noticed that sometimes the voice simply arrived in my head. *Touch me lightly here, touch me deeply here*, or *I'm crazy for my man, I'm tender for my child.* The first time I heard a voice shout, *ouch! Ow! Oh, the throb of life, the sting of it!* I jumped back from the couch, my hands raised in defence.

'Why've you stopped?' The guinea-pig student muttered.

'Sorry. Didn't you say ouch?'

Skin was speaking into my hands, like Braille under my fingers. Like a river, I never touch the same skin twice. Like a map, I could follow its intimacy.

The order and shape of each stroke creates a pattern that lasts for the entire massage. I try to maintain contact, so that my hands never stop, or lift from the skin, but move within their own memory. As the story builds, my hands tell it back. They know where to go, what to do. What to say. It's agonizing, but good; a singular giving. The stories flow into my body and linger there. Sometimes, I almost give myself away, asking about secrets I'd never been told. Sometimes I sob between clients. But there are shortcomings to every job. There are lots to being a shop assistant, and a load more to being a care assistant. A skin-load.

I wish I'd touched my ex more often. Maybe I would have guessed everything about him and packed and left before he broke me in so many ways.

I used deep pressure on Jordon, moving my thumbs and fingertips in tiny circles. My palms were flat upon the resisting surface, gliding across his shoulders, where the skin was scarlet and navy with intricate patterns. I heard him groan, but I didn't think he'd want me to ask if this was painful.

Hot breath moistens my face. The sound of wet throats. I see them running. All of them now. The sand-coloured troop in their heavy sand-covered boots and the helmets that are never strapped across the chin. They run for their lives, keeping together. They reach a ditch—an open sewer—and plough into it. The fetid liquid splashes up. Their shoulders are hunched, their knees bent. They make themselves small, these big men.

I hope they are heading for safety. I have felt the fear in them, but it's contradictory. I see Jordon glance behind, just once. His eyes are focused and intent, not mad with dread. This is his job. He is the recon. He sees, absorbs, concludes, reports. The job is full of fear, but he doesn't fear it. He just does it.

It's like a game. Like being 'it' on a team, or missing a go. Death is a game.

People, people like me, think the hardened warrior is a killing machine, but when my hands moved over Jordon, I understood. The hardened warrior is a surviving machine.

'You have a lot of knots and tension in your back,' I said.

'Yeah.'

'And in your neck. I'm going to work particularly on your neck and shoulders.'

He was silent for a moment. 'Yeah. It's the headaches. I thought a massage would help.'

'You didn't tell me you had headaches.'

His silence said, *what business was it of yours.*

'Okay,' I whispered. It's bad practice to engage clients in conversation once they are settled. They should become one with the massage. Then the odours seep into the brain and the sensation of hands send them trance-ward.

I moved his lower arms in turn, resting them over the kidney area so that I could slip my fingers right under his scapula. My hands worked on the trapezium, so named for it triangular shape but I always remembered it as the muscle most dragged out of shape if you dangle from your hands on a trapeze under a big top. I rested his arms back along his sides and started on the neck muscles. Here the tattoo separated into individual ribbons with fringed edges. My fingers stroked each muscle from sinew to sinew.

There is a smell of canvas and stale body sweat. There are regimented rows of bunks and on each of them a soldier lies in various states of undress and in various modes of occupation. Some sleep, some read. Some write laboriously onto lined A4 paper. One is wanking under a girlie mag. Some just stare at the curve of the bedsprings above them.

Jordon is lying on his side. He is reading a letter. He takes his time, tracing the message with his lips.

The opening to the tent swings. Someone arrives. The sun is so strong behind this person their silhouette disappears into the strength of the glare. Jordon glances up. He does not speak, but he folds the letter, fitting the pages precisely into the envelope and resealing the flap. He slides the letter under the pillow.

He has a mission. A job he must do. He knows it. He is a veteran now.

The veteran warrior differs from the hardened warrior in one thing. His luck. He has seen many fights, battles, excursions into enemy territory. He's been there when others were killed. Some enemy die—that is the hope. Some raw recruits will also fall—that is the way of things. But, from time to time, a hardened warrior goes down. The others will blame the slow supply of equipment and senior decisions that shaped the battle. Later on, they'll blame the futility of the war. But they will also say, *it was meant to be, it was his time.*

The veteran warrior is the one whose time is not up; he rises to seniority with troops under him. The veteran knows how an enemy thinks, uses stratagems and counterfeits to guess their next move and intercept it. The veteran makes very few mistakes. He may even, one day, retire to sit with grandchildren and show them the scars of war.

I had finished. Jordon's breath was quiet and even. For a moment, I'd offered him peace. As I washed my hands, I wondered about the mission. Did he take it? Was it dangerous? There were no visible healing wounds; he seemed unscathed. I dried my hands. Jordon breathed on. Quite without warning, the desire to know more overcame me. I longed to go back and start again, pull my hands over his story. Did he survive that final mission because he was a veteran? Was it a first test, the one that has defined his future? Or was he on leave, waiting for it to begin?

I crept out of the room, to let him wake naturally. On my return, he was dressed, strapping on a watch with an analogue face.

'I do hope that was beneficial.'

He hiked his fatigues by the Doberman belt. 'Great.'

'Maybe you'll want to make another appointment?'

'Can't, sorry.'

'You're a soldier?'

He grunted a reply.

'*Rise above*. What does that mean?'

'It's the motto of my regiment.'

'But what does it mean?'

'Whatcha mean, *mean*? What it says. You gotta rise above it.'

'But above what?'

He sniffed and considered. 'The pain, I guess.'

In the gap between clients, I write up my notes. I never include the stories skin tells me—never. I always stick to oils used, strokes found beneficial, and areas of tension. For Jordon, I scratch an X in the box titled *Date of Next Appointment*.

He's a veteran. He'll be okay.

I lock the door. I unzip the little white dress I always wear for my work. I ping my bra loose, kick off my clogs and wriggle out of my G string.

I pour the rest of Jordon's bottle of oil onto my palm. The little pool of oil smells medicinal. I watch it for a little while. There are no surface tremors. I must be ready for this, even though I had no idea.

I start with my feet. There are few muscles in the feet, but the skin there carries memories of all our travels. I finger the spaces between the metatarsals, circle the ankle bones, then work up—gastrocnemius, quadriceps, hamstrings, sartorius, gluteus. I run oiled fingers along the intercostals, over my breasts and across my shoulders. Bi's, tri's, pecs. I pull both hands behind my neck, searching out the deltoids, then upwards over the trapezius, feeling the stretch of the sternocleidomastoid, pushing into my face: triangularis, masseter, orbicularis, frontalis.

My hands and my history combine. A story of me I had never thought to ask.

I close my eyes and reach for my back.

A WORLD OF DIFFERENCE
Deborah Klée

IT is rare for a person to be sighted. A sighted person may not have a well-developed sense of smell. They may have difficulty hearing some pitches that are easily heard by non-sighted people. Their responses can, at times, be slow as they tend to lose concentration easily. This may be because they are distracted by sight.

The educational psychologist's words keep running through my mind. I need a cup of tea and time to think before Daniel gets home from school. The heady scent of a late flowering rose tells me I am at the garden gate. I trace my fingers over the house numbers, a habit now rather than a necessity as we have lived here for ten years. I love the sound of gravel crunching under my feet and the scent of lavender as I trail my hands across a pot at the front door. These familiar rituals help to still my mind.

It is a relief to kick off my shoes and momentarily sink my feet into the thick carpet before reaching the cool wooden floorboards of the kitchen. The kettle bleeps as it is filled and I sit down, ready now to face the truth that I have tried to ignore for the past thirteen years. My fingers trace the Braille, re-reading the words that have been playing through my mind. *It is rare for a person to be sighted.*

I always knew Daniel was special. It was hard at first; he was such a beautiful baby. I remember his warm sweet scent of milk and baby lotion as though it were yesterday. The soft, heavy weight of him in my arms.

The whistling kettle breaks into my thoughts, and I feel for the canister of Earl Grey. I like to use the loose-leaf tea in a diffuser spoon. There is a lovely fragrant flowery smell of bergamot as I pour the hot water over the spoon; a ping tells me the mug is full. It is this attention to each task that I cannot get Daniel to concentrate on. He is so impatient, his attention darting from one thing to another.

If I am honest, I know that he has not really settled into secondary school. It is so hard. I really want to keep him in a normal school but the psychologist says he is falling behind and a school for the sighted will help him catch up. There aren't many of these special schools as there is no real need. I have only met one other sighted person and that was years ago when I was a child. So Daniel would have to go away to the country and be a boarder during the week, and I don't know how he would cope living away from home. I have always kept him safe, stood up for him when kids called him names. People are so insensitive, talking about him as if he isn't there. He has developed a thick skin, but that is because he knows I am here for him. If he were away from home he may not be able to cope. I would miss him too. I cannot imagine living here on my own during the week. No Daniel to cook for, no dirty clothes to pick up from his bedroom floor. The clock says, in a deep male voice, that it is four thirty. Daniel is late home from school again. I must make a start on dinner. Spaghetti Bolognese, his favourite. I cannot put it off. I will have to talk to him tonight, see what he thinks.

It is nearly six when he finally gets home, banging the front door closed behind him. I wait for him to follow his nose to the kitchen where the spaghetti sauce is bubbling—rich with tomatoes, garlic and red wine. But no, he runs upstairs to his room, his feet playing a tune with each step. I wait for him to step up and down as he always does to play his tune and smile when he does. I know what he is up to. It is those damn flowers again. He is obsessed with collecting flowers and leaves and arranging them on a blank sheet. It is the colour that fascinates him, something that sighted people see, I guess. It is not something I understand. By mixing the flowers together he loses their individual scents.

'Daniel,' I call up the stairs. 'Dinner is ready.'

He appears moments later in the kitchen, sniffing the air and heading for the saucepan.

'My favourite, spaghetti! Thanks Mum.' He plants a kiss on my head to show off that he is now a head taller than me.

'Why are you so late Daniel? Have you been day dreaming by the river in the meadow again? '

He moves away from me, shuffling around by the table. 'Had to stay behind to talk to Mr Richards. He was going on about my reading and writing again. I can't use my fingers to read. I can't help it. Why can't I look at the shapes and patterns of the dots? I can still read.'

'Oh Daniel, you must learn to read Braille the right way. Your way is too slow.' This is exactly what the psychologist was telling me. He is getting behind in his studies.

'I wish I wasn't sighted! If I couldn't see, it would not matter that the world is drab and grey. Why can't we dress to look like the flowers? Everything is the same dull colour, even my clothes and my room!'

We have had this discussion a million times. I have tried everything. His wall paper has a raised pattern of sweets. Their scent has long disappeared but when he was a little boy he loved feeling and smelling them. I had to stop him from pulling them off the wall to eat! I used all of my savings to make his room special, to make up for his problems. He has a thick shaggy rug in the middle of the floor. He even named it Freddy Bear. I hung a glass mobile in the window. It tinkles in the wind but Daniel likes it because he says it catches the light and makes rainbows on the wall. It is never enough. He always goes back to the lack of colour in his world. I do not want to broach the subject of the special school for the sighted until after dinner. Why spoil his favourite meal?

However, it cannot be put off forever and when Daniel is clearing away our plates, I decide to approach the subject.

'Come and sit down when you have done that, love. There is something that I need to talk to you about.'

I take out the letter and smooth it flat on the table. Daniel sighs heavily, something that he has been doing a lot since he turned thirteen.

'Will it take long? I have things to do,' he grumbles, settling into the chair next to me.

I tell him about my summons to the educational psychologist. That the psychologist is concerned that he is disadvantaged by attending a normal school, and that his special needs are not being met.

'What special needs?' he sounds angry and defensive.

'Well love, you have trouble concentrating because you are distracted by your sight.' I start but he interrupts.

'It is all of the sound and smells that are distracting, not my sight! I walk along the street and all I hear is the noise of people's watches telling the time, the town clock sounding every fifteen minutes, people's sticks tapping and those new talking canes. Then there are the trams and cars honking and announcing their programmed route. If people could see they would not have to make noise all the time. That is just the sound! What about the smells? The bread smell that is pumped out of the bakery, the coffee from the deli and leather from the shoe shop? The plants on every street corner, lavender, thyme, roses!'

'If we did not have flowers and shrubs planted in the streets we would not know where we were going. How would I know where the bread shop is without the smell?' I try to understand him, really I do, but sometimes he makes no sense.

'That is what I am trying to say!' He is all worked up now. 'If people could see they would not need the sounds and smells, would they?'

I stroke his hair and try to calm him. 'Don't be silly sweetheart. How would we get on if all of us were sighted? It is a nice dream but it would not work and it is not going to happen. But—' I brace myself to introduce the idea of a school for the sighted. 'There is a school where all of the pupils are sighted.'

He is quiet and I do not know whether he is shocked or just thinking. 'It is only an idea love. You do not have to go if you don't want to.'

He is still quiet and I long to pull him onto my knee like I did when he was tiny, and I could feel his mood through his body—but he is nearly a man now. Instead, I reach out for his hand. Surprisingly, he does not pull it away.

'It is in the countryside, darling. You would have to board there from Monday to Friday.'

He squeezes my hand. 'Let's go and have a look Mum. If I don't like it I won't have to go there, will I?'

'Of course not, darling.' I am relieved that he has taken it so well. He jumps up and heads off to his bedroom. Back to those flowers and leaves. His room is full of papers with flowers attached to them in patterns. Just one of the reasons I am not allowed in there anymore.

We only had to wait a couple of weeks for an appointment to visit The Stannah School for the Sighted. The wait feels longer though; I am worried and can think of nothing else. It could really change our lives and I do not know if it would be for the better. It is at times like this that it is hard being a single parent. His father is no help, he did a runner as soon as he realised there was something wrong with Daniel. We have not heard from him since.

Daniel is quiet. I have had little more than grunts and sighs from him this morning, but that is his usual vocabulary these days. I try to reassure him.

'We are only having a look, love. You do not have to go there. We can get you extra tuition in the holidays, help you catch up, if you want to stay where you are.'

He grunts and I try to distract myself by reading a magazine.

The first thing that hits me when we walk into the school is the stillness and lack of scent. It is disorientating as the door does not bleep when we open it, and there is no announcement to tell us where we are. Instead, a voice carries from a corner of the room.

'You must be Daniel. If you wait here a moment Mrs Fellows will be with you shortly.'

Daniel takes my arm and guides me into an armchair. I have always prided myself on not needing a stick, but in this school there is nothing to tell me where I am. I expect it is just because it is new to us.

Daniel gasps in wonder. 'Mum, it's beautiful! The carpet is like the meadow and the walls are like the different flowers, the buttercups and cow parsley. It's amazing.' I can hear the joy and wonder in his voice. He gasps again and I am thankful when he clutches my hand. 'She has hair like golden wheat and a dress of cornflowers!'

I hear people approaching us and stand up. My hand is taken in a firm handshake, and I smell a pleasant spicy scent of good perfume.

'Hello, Mrs Johnson, and you must be Daniel. This is Jessica, a pupil here; she is going to show you around Daniel, while I talk to your mother.' So Jessica is the owner of the wheat hair and cornflower dress, I smile to myself.

Once they have gone, Mrs Fellows takes my arm and guides me along the corridor. I have to say it does not feel comfortable being led but there doesn't seem to be another option. She must sense my discomfort because she says, 'We do not have musical floor tiles or textured walls. We do not have speaking clocks or scented rooms. We want our students to use their eyes. You may find it difficult to find your way around.'

I nod and follow her lead until we are sitting comfortably in her office. She orders some tea and we settle down. I have so much to ask and hope that we have time to talk properly before Daniel joins us.

'We encourage our students to use their sight and think of it as an asset, a gift,' Mrs Fellows starts.

'I agree,' I say. 'I have always told Daniel that he is special and his sight is a gift, but he has to learn how to live in a world that is not sighted. I am worried that if he comes here, he will not be able to fit in when he leaves.'

We are interrupted as the tea arrives. Again I feel helpless as my tea is poured for me and placed in my hand as if I am disabled. I wonder whether Mrs Fellows is sighted and ask gently so as not to cause offence.

'Yes, I have been sighted since birth but do not see it as a disability.' She pauses to sip her tea then goes on. 'We create an environment where sighted young people feel comfortable and able to concentrate on their studies. We have an excellent success rate.'

I am not convinced. It all feels strange, so different from what Daniel is used to. I try to explain my concerns.

'I would like him to develop his sense of smell, touch, taste and hearing. I do not want him to be distracted by his sight.'

'Of course, most parents who do not have sight feel the same way. We have a meditation class twice a week where we teach pupils to block out any distractions. This includes sight and noise. A sighted person can find the sounds of daily life overwhelming at times. It is not just their sight that distracts them.'

I still have many questions but we are interrupted as Daniel and Jessica burst into the room laughing. I can feel Daniel's energy and excitement; it fills the room.

'Mum, it's brilliant. There is a room where we can use colours to make pictures and we can make our clothes different colours!'

I do not understand but Mrs Fellows explains. 'We make up paints and dyes using the natural colours from plants. Our students enjoy using colour in their creative studies.'

I am surprised that they are encouraging this pointless activity and say so. 'That is all I ever hear about from Daniel, he is obsessed with colour.'

'We find that most of our students appreciate colour, but once they know how to create it and use it, colour becomes common place,' Mrs Fellows answers.

I can tell that Daniel is enthusiastic, but I am still worried.

'What happens to your students when they leave here?' I ask.

'They are better equipped to deal with the world as they leave here with more confidence. They go into many different jobs as they usually leave with good qualifications. The majority settle back into the communities they came from, but some prefer to live in communities of sighted people.'

I touch Daniel's face and feel his broad smile. The realization that he is growing up and will be leaving me hurts. It is like my insides are being pulled out and the cord that has bound us since birth is being severed. They are all waiting for me to say something, to ask Daniel what he thinks, but I can't. Instead I say, 'We need to go away and have a think.'

'Of course, let me show you out,' Mrs Fellows stands up. 'Here are some leaflets for you to take away with you,' she gives these to Daniel.

'What are the marks on these ones?' he asks.

'That is writing,' Mrs Fellows explains 'We teach you how to read and write the written word as well as using Braille.'

This is too much. Daniel has a lot of catching up to do, learning a useless skill will waste his time. I have to say something. 'What use is that? Only sighted people can read and write the written word.'

Again, Mrs Fellows has an answer. She must be used to parents like me.

'We use both. The written word is easier for sighted people to read than Braille and it helps them to progress more quickly with their studies. We insist that they continue to use Braille and improve their reading and writing.'

I cannot argue with that. Daniel needs to improve his reading and writing, and he has been struggling with Braille. It kind of makes sense. I shake Mrs Fellow's hand and tell her we will be in touch.

Daniel doesn't stop talking all the way home. I feel as though I travelled in with one boy and returned with an entirely different one. When we get home I sit him down.

'What do you want to do Daniel?'

He doesn't reply straight away and I am grateful. For just a moment I can hope, but I know in my heart that the school will be good for him.

'I don't know, Mum. I don't want to leave you.' He takes my hand, bless him.

'You could come home every weekend,' I say but my voice is hoarse with emotion.

'Will you be alright without me?' he puts his arm around me.

'Of course I will be alright!' I put on a good face. I don't want him to feel responsible for me.

'Then I would like to give it a go.' I can hear the excitement in his voice. 'When would I start?'

Until today I had not realized how different Daniel's needs are to mine. I am afraid that our differences will start to pull us apart and so I say, 'Maybe one day we will have a world where the sighted and non-sighted can live together without either feeling at a disadvantage.'

'Wouldn't that be amazing?' he replies. 'Maybe we could help to make that happen.'

COCKLE SHELLS
Simone Davy

I'M splashing through the water, my arms are paddles—here comes a wave. Oh, it's a big one, crashing over my head. I'm falling. The float is above me; its clown face is grinning, laughing that I had to let go. Mummy wasn't near enough to help. I'm going down. I'm a jug filling with water. *Byeeeeeee.* Where am I going? Long ribbons curl around my legs. I'm freezing cold. Where has the sun gone? I don't like it down here. I want to get out. *Help!*

Two large hands are pulling me up and out of the water. Splutter, cough, hiccup—there's a salty taste on my lips. I'm safe, the sun is warm on my back; I blink and the sea water stings my eyes. Then I'm sick, right into the water. It's glued to my hair, and some of the stuff is running down my new Muppets swimsuit that I got for my birthday. I'm seven now. I can taste salmon paste sandwiches and seaweed. Spit it out quick. I'm dribbling like my dog Timmy.

'Mummy!' I cry.

'It's all right, I've got you. You just went under for a bit. Come now, you're OK, just been a bit sick.' We paddle through the shallows. She takes off her candy floss pink scarf and gives it to me; it flies up in the air like a kite.

'Here, blow your nose, Janie.'

I blow as hard as I can. I've got the whole of the sea up there. The scarf is nice. It smells of suntan oil. I've messed it up, but she doesn't care.

'It looks like you've got jellyfish legs.'

'What are they, Mummy?' I hold her hand tightly. I don't want to fall over.

'They are legs that are all cold and shivery.'

'Oh.' The water in my ears makes everything move from side to side as if I'm in a tunnel. I'd like to be carried, but I'm too heavy now. I'm brave until I get to the pebbles which are sharp and hard under my toes, and I start to cry. Tears and snot pour out. I wonder if this is what it is like inside me.

Mummy picks up a shell and places it carefully in my hand.

'Look, Janie, it's a cockle shell, like in the nursery rhyme.' I like the feel of it. It has a rainbow on the outside and inside it's smooth where the creature used to live. I bet it was happy in there. As we walk up the beach, I hold the shell tightly in my hand. I'm going to keep it forever.

'Come on, we're nearly there. Would you like an Orange Maid?'

My favourite. I nod.

'I'm going to have a lemon sorbet,' she says.

She buys me the lolly and we go back to our towels. I stick out my tongue and show Mummy how it has turned bright orange. I can't wait to read the joke on the wooden stick. It always makes us laugh.

'Oh no, Mummy, I've lost my shell.' I start to cry again.

'It doesn't matter, love, finish your lolly and we'll go and find some more,' she strokes my hair as she finishes her ice-cream.

Nowadays I feel almost grown-up. I phone home on Sunday nights and Mum sends me letters with recipes, news and sometimes a ten pound note.

I spin round. The lights are flashing in my eyes. I spin some more. The sounds of the guitars fill my ears, and the dance floor seems to shift. Everyone is everywhere. The chorus goes on and I wonder if I can keep up, keep dancing until it ends. The Levellers play and I sing. I imagine I'm in the band; the music loud in my ears, the microphone in my hands and students whirling around in front of me.

The taste of cider reminds me of home. Suddenly I'm thinking of Mum, missing the apples that she bakes in their skins, hot currants, brown sugar and honey oozing out. I wonder what they had for tea. They will be in bed now: Mum reading a novel with the bedside light on, and Dad asleep next to her.

More dancing—I'm tripping over the length of my skirt. It's made of layers of gold and silver sewn by her hands; no-one else has one like it. Adam tells me it's like dancing with a queen. We met a whole week ago, but it feels more like a year. We're sweeping the floor of cans and cigarette butts with our feet. The soles of my black suede boots are slippery from spilt lager.

He grabs my hand and I laugh, he spins me round faster and we fall into one another. At last the song ends and we slip down onto the floor, backs against the wall. He lights a cigarette, the smoke spiralling upwards. I put my head on his shoulder and breathe in the scent of the smoke. It mingles with the incense coming from the stage. We watch our friends dancing in a circle with their arms wrapped round each other. We laugh as the lead singer jumps off the stage, throwing his cap in the air.

'Are you going home for the holidays, Janie?' He doesn't look at me as he stubs out his cigarette.

'Yes, you?'

'No, there's no point. I'd rather stay here.' I like the way his hair falls over his face.

I think of hot apples, baths with lavender oil and a bed with sheets made crisp and clean. Space to dream.

Mum and I used to love shopping together, but now I go alone. I haven't been inside this secondhand shop before. An icy arm tries to pull me back but as I open the door the warmth of the shop wraps around me. I can smell old clothes and the shelves are brimming with ornaments and books. This is the bit I like, looking and touching the objects. I hope I will find something. I breathe in the smell, musty like Mum's old shoe boxes at the back of the wardrobe. If I find something that reminds me of her, I will feel calmer.

'Excuse me dear.' A woman rummaging through a basket of scarves knocks my arm and apologises.

'That's all right, there is so much in here, isn't there?' I say. We smile politely. I wonder what she is looking for; maybe she too is looking for pictures of her past.

I scan the shelves. I see a figurine, a woman with a long sweeping skirt, lilac and mauve. Behind her is a cut glass vase. Mum had one of those. It sat on the dining table, sometimes empty, sometimes full. Scent of lilac from the garden in spring and roses in the summer. I take it down and run my finger over the sharp diagonals. It would sit nicely on my bedroom windowsill, the light catching the glass.

I can't resist staying in the shop a little longer. It would be better to leave, but I like the look of the secondhand rail. The feel of the old clothes is soothing; they have already lived. The red cardigan would have suited her. I slip it off the hanger and let it fall loosely around my shoulders. In the full length mirror my face is serious. I must leave now. I am always strict with myself, only two items per shop.

I take the vase and cardigan to the woman at the desk.

'I've been hoping someone would buy that vase. It's been sitting there forever. I like cut glass but it's not popular anymore, is it?'

'No, I guess not.' I pass the woman a handful of change. She takes the vase and carefully places it in a bag; I let the red cardigan fall and wrap the vase.

As I walk down the high street, I feel cold as though I'm walking though sea spray. I feel the eyes of the Saturday shoppers on me. They think I'm just an ordinary young woman, and I shiver.

Mum was beautiful. Wavy long hair, chestnut brown, that couldn't be tamed by plaits or pins. As a treat on a Saturday night she would let me curl her hair with tongs. I would sit cross-legged in front of the electric fire. Sometimes I left them on for too long, and the strands would be scorched and smell of burnt toast. She would laugh and scold me.

I'm almost back to the car now. I'm safe, though once I'm home and the vase is on the windowsill I know how I will feel. Images of losing her will wash over me again.

When he sees my bag, Adam will ask if I have bought more things. He is angry that the wardrobe contains more old clothes than new. He will go and talk to Dad on the phone. Dad will ask what I've brought home this time. All he has in his flat is a wedding photo and a landscape she painted of the mountains around Apple Cross. His grief is so quiet I can hardly hear it, but if I listen carefully it is there, lingering between his words.

Adam doesn't understand why I need more things—he says it's been long enough. I tell him that grief lasts forever. I can't look at a photograph of Mum, but I can touch, breath in and look at these things I have collected. I draw memories around me as if they are thick, blue velvet curtains closing in on the dark.

I sit in the car and look at myself in the mirror. I look older than I should, and I don't look like anyone I know. The only things I recognise in my face are my eyes; I can see the pure blue of her eyes in mine. They are so bright they make me think of the sea and the sky on a Cornish beach.

As I turn the ignition, I'm startled. There is a kicking inside me, a movement as though butterflies are there. I begin to feel lighter as though I too have wings.

We are lying on large blue beach towels. I have a book, Adam has a Kindle. I turn pages whilst he touches the screen. The sun is getting too hot, so I sit up and stroke his back. He turns over and sprinkles my feet with sand.

'Come on, Janie, lets race to the sea,' he shouts. Already he is running down the beach.

'I'm getting too big for chasing you around.' I follow him, holding the bump—it is quite large now. I struggle, laughing and almost falling over.

At last I get to the sea and he pulls me in to where it is deep. The sea is calm today—just right. There is the taste of salt on my lips. I swim and the water makes me feel light, the weight of her lost in the water. I roll onto my back, close my eyes and listen to the seagulls screeching above me.

Being here reminds me of Mum. I can see her walking down the beach with a turquoise sarong around her waist and a large sun hat shading her eyes. She said I was going to be the fastest swimmer in the world, the tallest girl in the class and the brightest button in the box. I'm going to say the same things to my girl. I roll back over and swim to shore. Adam's got bored waiting. I can see him sunbathing—he knows how much I love the sea.

As I walk back up the beach, I see shells lying on the shoreline. I bend slowly and pick up the prettiest ones, the waves lapping over my hands.

'I'll put them on your windowsill,' I say to my baby girl, as I hold the shells in the palm of my hand.

'If you keep them forever, you will always have the sea close by.'

The continuous tides pass back and forth across the sand.

WHEN THE WIND CHANGES
Debz Hobbs-Wyatt

ROBERT scoops snow into his glove. He shapes it, pats it down and presses it into the face of the snowman. I'm not sure what it's supposed to be, a nose perhaps, but everyone knows a carrot is best for that. He's been building the snowman for twenty minutes, working systematically, rolling the body, then the head, placing twigs where its fingers are supposed to be. He only looked up once when the cat ran along the fence, Bill Broad's big black cat. He steps back and I see his face. He's remembering me.

He's remembering the last time we built a snowman and Dad took a photograph of us. Robert has the photograph now. He took it from my room. They tell one another that they never go in there, they *can't* go in there. But they do. I've seen Mum with her face pressed into my dressing gown, as if she thinks she can fold herself into it and disappear. I've seen her running her fingers across my things, so lightly she's afraid if she presses too hard something will break. Or maybe she's afraid *she* will break.

Nan doesn't go in. I see her standing in the doorway thinking she sees me. Telling me she forgives me. Mum says she's just a crazy old woman, but I know she's not.

When Robert took the photograph from my room I was there, willing him to see me the way Nan does. He keeps the picture in a shoebox. It's where he keeps all the things that remind him of me. I suppose that's all that's left in the end. A shoebox with random things like the notebook where I scribbled ideas about what I wanted to be; dog-eared football cards; a Rubik's cube with half the stickers missing; and a photograph of me and my brother standing next to a snowman.

In the photograph I'm wearing my red hat, the one with the flaps that used to cover my ears. One of Nan's lopsided creations because she never could get it right, knit one, purl two, or something like that. 'Arthritic hands,' she'd say and Mum would smile, laughter spreading out like sunshine in the delicate lines on her face.

The red hat is the same red hat they found with my things. It's how they knew where I was.

Robert turns his head in my direction and I see his cheeks are wet. He thinks if anyone sees they'll blame the wind. It's what he tells himself. *Twelve year old boys aren't supposed to cry.* It's what Kevin Ash used to say to me. And it's the words Robert pushes into his pillow because there are some words he can't say out loud.

Pillows are where we hide all our secrets.

Robert doesn't cry so much anymore, but he'll cry today. It's been a year. A year since it happened. That means I'll have to go soon. I'm ready now. It's time to stop crying.

It's true what people say. They say things get easier and time heals. They say these things all the time; the teachers, the neighbours, the people in the office where Mum works, the men at Dad's factory. And they all wear the same expression but I know what they're thinking. They're thinking, *thank God it didn't happen to us*, and when they think about me they hold onto their children, a little tighter, a little longer—because you just never know.

I certainly didn't know what I was going to do that day. Until then nothing had ever happened, not really. It's like no one saw me. Except, that is, for Kevin Ash.

The shotgun belonged to Bill Broad. I found it when I was helping clear out his shed the summer before. It was just lying there on a shelf behind jars of nails, old paint, and a tin of bullets. I can remember the feel of it under my fingertips. I can remember its outline in the dust; but I never meant to take it. I never meant for anything to happen.

I stand by the fence looking at my brother and I don't want him to go through what I did. Kevin Ash said something to Robert once, so I promised him that I'd always protect him. As I watch him now, pressing stones into the front of the snowman, I realise I don't want things to change. I don't want my little brother to forget me. I suppose there will always be a shoebox and a photograph. But one day even those will be gone. 'When the wind changes,' Bill Broad used to say, 'snowmen melt'.

I imagine a spot on the grass, a carrot, a few twigs, a hat. It seems so sad, as if that would be all that's left; nothing else to show where we were except, maybe, a photograph.

I watch the house on the corner where Melanie Banks stands at the window, running her hands along the edge of the curtain. Today her hair is pulled back. She's looking into the street. Mel was in my class, she was there that day. She was there another day too, in the street when Kevin Ash and the others had me on the ground. She pretended not to see but I know she did. She turns her head now, watches my brother as he drapes Dad's orange scarf around the snowman's neck—another of Nan's knit one, purl five accidents. Mel watches, thinking about me. She remembers the time I kissed her and she wonders how something so nice could feel so wrong. Then she wonders if she'd let me kiss her again, if she could have changed anything. For a long time Mel had nightmares, thinking she should have said something, told Mr Graham what she'd seen. And she thinks about what would have happened if I had pulled the trigger, if I had killed Kevin Ash, or any of them. But that's just it—I couldn't do it, not even after what he did to Bill Broad.

I suppose I was the only one who had time for Bill Broad. Mum said, her voice always lowered, that he had mental problems and, from time to time, had to be sectioned.

To me, he was just a kind old man. He didn't mean any harm and spent most of his time planting, watering and digging up vegetables. He gave Mum a whole bag of potatoes once. But Dad said we shouldn't accept them, as if they were tainted or something, like he had a disease that would rub off. I couldn't take them back though, and so the whole lot rotted. I never did tell Bill.

He was always talking about the weather too.

'Wind is changing again, Jason,' he'd say. 'When the wind changes you never know what it might bring.'

It's what he said to me that day.

Kevin Ash is the one that killed Bill's dog. It was a terrible thing. I can still see her face, sweet little Millie. I can still hear Kevin Ash's laugh. It was poison. He fed it to her right there in the street. She was so trusting.

Sometimes now I stand over Kevin Ash as he sleeps. I call his name; wake him so he looks right into my eyes.

'Fifteen-year-olds aren't supposed to wet the bed,' I say. I don't just say it once. I repeat it over and over, the way he did to me. I know it's wrong.

Kevin still has nightmares about that day, me standing in the middle of Mr Graham's math class, pointing Bill's shotgun at him. It was the day he killed the dog and I was out of my mind on half a bottle of Dad's home-brewed cider. It was the first time I'd ever gotten drunk.

I don't know how it happened, things had built up. What he did to sweet little Millie—that finally broke me. She was just a beautiful happy thing. I suppose she still is.

Mel's dad joins her at the window. He tells her she doesn't have to go if she doesn't want to. She sweeps a hair from her eyes.

'I have to. We *all* do,' she says.

He nods, doesn't say anything.

There's movement all along the street. Some people I know from school and some I don't, but they all know who I am. They're coming outside, wrapped up in their winter coats, little ones with mittens dangling on strings. I think of Nan and how she used to make the same kind of mittens for us.

Robert turns his head towards Mum. She stands in the open doorway and pushes her hands into knitted gloves, the left one too big, the right one too small. The gloves Nan had me wrap up for her one Christmas.

'Oh, they're perfect,' she'd said. When Nan wasn't looking she winked and we both laughed head-back-belly-laughs that only we understood.

Now Mum is looking at all the people. She can't believe how many there are.

Some of them walk on the road, others move along the pavement. All of them turn to look at our house. No one speaks, but a dog barks somewhere.

Mel walks arm in arm with her dad. I don't see my dad but I know where he is. He's in my room and he's wondering when they'll be strong enough to take everything away, to accept that I'm not coming back.

'Another day,' he mouths. 'Not today.'

I am sure he will do it one day, but I'll be gone and I won't have to see.

Dad watches Mum and Robert from the window. They're waiting for him. He sees the snowman, wonders where the photo is; the one he took of me and my brother. He'll search until it drives him crazy, the way everything drives him crazy: like thinking about why his son got drunk and walked into school brandishing a shotgun. He asks himself why his son then ran away and blew his brains out. He wonders why he did it by the lake where no one would find him for two days.

Mr Graham stands outside his house on the other side of town and pulls his coat tighter. When he thinks about me, he thinks about Kevin Ash and wonders if he could have done something to stop it.

But it's not Mr Graham's fault.

I watch them making their way towards the lake. Bill Broad is there. He walks behind, keeping his distance from Dad although in time I know even Dad will forgive him. It's not his fault. Bill walks folded over, shuffling his feet in a way that leaves lines in the snow. He blames himself for the gun. I wish he could hear me. I wish he knew how I sat with him after it happened, him with his head in his hands. I told him what really happened. I told him it wasn't his fault and I told him it was like something just snapped. I told him they shouldn't have killed his dog. Harry Parkes, the local bobby, called it the final straw. He said it happens to kids who are bullied. I figured Bill would understand that, he knew all about bullies. He'd been bullied his whole life.

I cross the street as we get close to the lake and I continue to watch them. Mum, Dad, Robert, Nan. They can't believe so many have come.

Dad takes one of the tea lights from his pocket and lights it with an unsteady hand. He places it on the ground. It is a few feet from where I died, one insane moment I can never take back—a drunken stumble, a shotgun without a safety catch. I still see their faces the day Harry Parkes came round and showed them my hat.

And then Dad showed him the photograph.

Mum lights her candle. She whispers the Lord's Prayer even though she no longer believes in God. Then it's Robert's turn. He seems to look right at me and for a second I wonder, but then he turns away.

Mel lifts her head, says my name. She's remembering the kiss. *I should have let you kiss me again*, she thinks.

'Yes,' I say. 'I'd wished for that.' She hears me and lifts her head to the wind, but it's only as a thought, fragile as a breath, then it's gone.

Everyone lights candles. I think I can hear singing, but it's not the crowd; sweet voices drift toward me from across the lake. Mr Graham steps forwards, takes a piece of paper from his pocket. When he speaks his voice breaks so I go to him, hold his arm until I feel him relax.

'One year on,' he says. 'Thank you all for coming. Jason would be proud.'

'I am,' I say. Then I think I see something, it comes from across the lake where the singing seems to grow louder.

'It's up to all of us,' Mr Graham says, 'to remember.' He looks in Dad's direction. 'And to talk about it.'

That's when I see Tom Hart from the Gazette. He scribbles something in his notebook. I see Dad standing between Nan and Mum. I see Bill light his candle.

'I miss you Bill,' I whisper. For a second he lifts his head, the wind coaxing tears. I see him look down. Something moves at his feet.

I walk to the edge of the water and look across. I think at first it's a reflection, a hundred candles quavering in the ripple. But it's not. It is much brighter than that.

I feel a rush of air, something moving towards me. Just before I leave, I take one last look.

'Don't forget me,' I say. 'Especially you, Robert.'

The wind changes. Flames bend over, smearing golden arcs across the blackness. Bill tilts his head, looks across the water. Robert looks up.

As I go they think they see something. They think they see a boy and a dog.

Got You
Amy Hulsey

He's dumb. The road we usually sleep on is closed for construction and Dad is looking at me like it's my fault, his eyebrows lost in his dirty bangs. Our habitual alleyway is blocked off by orange cones and men in matching vests. We walk past men in hard hats, huge yellow machines, and honking cars driven by clean-shaven but suddenly dishevelled businessmen. Dad watches the construction workers like it was their idea to revamp this particular avenue.

'I'm tired,' I say. It's true. My feet hurt.

Dad, dumb as ever, turns his greasy brown eyes on me. He puts a hand in my hair and, under the guise of a father rustling his son's shaggy hair, pulls out a handful.

'Shut up and keep walking.'

I look back over my shoulder and the sticky strands clutch with dirt and oil on the sidewalk. It's hard to tell how much hair as the world is multiplied and muggy through my watery eyes. My scalp burns. It feels a little wet right at the top. I'd touch it if Dad wasn't watching my every move. Hair dangles from the fingernail of his index finger.

A woman stares out her windshield at me. I want to wipe my eyes, but she would think I'm crying. Her lips are bright red. They match her hair. I want to break her windshield. It's cold. I want her to feel it. I want to rip at her hair and make the wind blow right in her eyes so she knows that I'm not crying.

We pass the traffic and the roadworks. Dad looks down side streets and alleys. The wind is crazy and my toes are numb. His hair whips around like angry snakes.

An empty car is parked halfway on the sidewalk ahead of us. When we get close to it, Dad kicks it hard. He screams. He's not hurt; it's not that kind of scream. He's angry and stupid and his teeth are bared. He looks like a rabid dog. The car doesn't scream back and that makes Dad angrier. He kicks the car again.

The front of his shoe tears; his ugly big toe sticks out of his sock. I can see his uncut toenail from where I am, standing next to him in front of the banged up car.

A woman walking towards us crosses the street, as if we're going to attack her. She makes eye contact with me and tries to smile. She looks scared. Dad grabs my wrist and pulls me around the car. The woman watches with wide eyes and a scrunched up fake smile. She's almost jogging in her tight skirt and heels. If Dad saw her he probably would have barked at her. He's been angry like this for as long as I can remember. I think that's why my mother left him with me. He was probably always angry at her for no reason. Either that or she noticed how stupid he was.

When we're around the car, Dad doesn't let go. His long fingers grip me tighter. His bones rub against my bones and I can almost hear them scraping together like two stones. I might catch fire.

'Ow!' I say, because my wrist is going to bruise. Dad walks faster. His broken shoe makes a sad flopping sound with every other step. It blends with the honking horns of the traffic that I can still see if I turn around. The woman in the skirt and heels passes the orange cones. She passes the alley that is my bedroom. Anyone watching would know that the woman is running away from us—unless maybe they're dumb too.

'Hurry up,' Dad says. I run to keep up with him. My stomach hurts. I haven't eaten in a day and a half. Before that, it was a piece of bread and half a can of cold soup that he grudgingly shared with me.

'Dad, slow down.' I'm whining. I know it'll make him even madder, but I keep pulling against his hand and whining. 'I'm hungry, Dad.' He pulls harder on my arm and continues on. 'My feet hurt.'

'Shut up,' he says. He doesn't even look at me, just watches his feet move.

'But *Da-aad*.' I sound like I'm six years old. Dad's grip tightens. Our bones grind together and I can definitely feel sparks igniting.

He stops. I half run into him and fall down. He doesn't let go of my wrist and my arm twists. 'Are you done?' he asks.

Dad lets go of my wrist and I fall the rest of the way to the cement. I pull my arm to my chest and curl my body around it. My wrist looks angry and red; swelling like a hot balloon. My shoulder is weak and wobbly.

'Get up,' Dad says. He kicks my back with his still-whole shoe. It's not a hard kick, but it jostles my wrist enough to hurt. 'Now.'

I stand up. Dad doesn't help me. He just stands there with his arms crossed. I get to my feet without using my hands because I have to cradle my arm. I think it will fall off at the shoulder if I don't hold it in place.

'Let's go.' Dad starts walking as soon as I get on my feet. He slows his pace though, and that makes it easier. I follow him with my head down, watching his heels move and his pants flap about his legs. The top of my head still feels wet and my wrist and arm throb, as if Dad threw half of me into a fire.

We walk. I don't know where we're going. I doubt Dad does, either. He's probably just wandering around until he finds somewhere we can sleep.

We turn a corner. A man in a dirty apron sits on a milk crate smoking a cigarette. Dad turns us back and we hide behind the building.

'Go get us some dinner,' he says, pushing me around the corner.

My feet slap against the pavement and the smoking man looks up at me. He exhales in a huge puff of white.

'Hey, kiddo,' he says. 'What you doing out? It's gettin' dark.'

'I know,' I say, holding my elbow tight against my side.

'You should head home,' he says.

'Got none,' I shrug.

The smoking man throws his cigarette on the ground. He stands up and pulls down his apron. 'Stay here,' he says and disappears through the door.

I stand outside for a few minutes. When he returns, he's got a cup of something hot and a plastic bag filled with paper-wrapped food. It smells fantastic and warm. The man looks at the closed door behind him.

'Take this. You gotta eat something.' He pushes the bag at me. I loop the handles around my good wrist and take the coffee in my hand. The man looks at my arm.

'I don't wanna see you here again. I don't need this kind of trouble.'

Dad comes around the corner and nods.

The man pulls a knife out of his apron and shouts, 'Get outta here! I don't need you and your little boyfriend trying to rob me or get me fired. Get lost!'

Dad pulls on the back of my shirt and backs away with his other hand in the air. 'We just need some dinner. Don't get crazy.'

The man swings his knife around in front of him. It's scarier that Dad is backing away and trying to talk nice. He will blame me for this.

We walk away with our food and a cup of hot coffee. Dad hits the back of my head.

'You almost got us killed!'

'It wasn't my fault,' I say, clutching the coffee so Dad can't take it away from me. 'You made me talk to him.'

Dad grabs the bag and digs through it.

'Burritos.' It's the first time I've seen Dad smile in a while. It's like I brought him a bag of money. He sits down on a curb and digs in. I sip the coffee. It's the warmest thing I've ever felt. My throat burns from it. When I reach for the bag to get my own burrito, Dad hits my hand away.

'Get dinner without almost getting us killed; then you can eat.'

I'm getting bigger. In a couple months I'll be thirteen. Dad knows what that means. It means that women will not give me free things anymore, because I'm not as cute as I was when I was ten. It means that I will start getting knives pointed at me.

'I got us that!' I yell. The cement of the curb is cold through my pants. It's not quite dark yet. I can see the cheese in the burrito Dad swallows down; I imagine the sun wrapped in the warmest blanket.

Dad takes a big bite and chews with his mouth open. I watch him eat. I don't drink any more coffee because it'll make me sick. I set the cup down next to Dad. He picks it up right away and empties it into his messy mouth.

There are three more burritos in the bag. I don't hope to get one, but it would be nice.

Dad stands up and takes the burritos with him. I stand up and wait for him to start walking. My legs are jelly underneath me, but they hold me up. Dad walks into the next park he finds and settles behind a bush. I follow him and wait for him to unroll our sleeping bag.

'Get in,' he mumbles after he has climbed in. I struggle to squeeze in next to him without bumping my wrist or shoulder.

I would toss and turn but the sleeping bag is small and Dad is big and I'm getting bigger. The sleeping bag stretches tighter every night, despite the fact that I shouldn't be growing because I'm not eating. I'm exhausted, but my stomach hurts and my arm hurts. My stomach aches in a way that feels like more than just hunger.

Dad kicks in his sleep. He never takes his shoes off, so his kicks are hard. Even with his worn out shoes, my legs feel battered by the middle of the night. My nose goes numb because it's sticking out of the sleeping bag. Eventually Dad stops kicking and starts using his hands instead. He grabs at my hair or my throat. His fingers try to wrap around something. They reach around my chest and pull at the front of my shirt. The fabric pulls at my shoulder. I want to scream but don't dare wake him.

I let Dad hit me in his sleep. There's nothing else I can do. Something else wakes Dad, because his eyes are open and he's staring straight at my face. He's got that stupid mean dog look on his face again.

Dad sits up, taking me with him. We're cocooned together like Siamese twins. 'Get out,' he says.

I climb out of the sleeping bag, shivering, and wait for Dad to lie back down. When he doesn't, I ask if I can get back in.

'No. You're sleeping out there tonight. You almost got me killed.'

So now he's going to try to kill me. My jacket isn't warm enough for frozen nights like tonight. There is no fat on my body to keep me warm. I huddle myself into the smallest ball I can and wait for my legs to go numb. My fingers are freezing. The cold feels good on my swollen wrist, but it hurts the rest of me.

Dad lies back down in the warm sleeping bag and goes back to sleep. He snores. My teeth chatter so I clench my jaw. I can't wake Dad. He would kill me with his own hands instead of giving me a chance to not freeze to death.

Dad knows what it means that I'm getting bigger. We'll have to get another sleeping bag. I'll have to eat more. People will start asking why I'm not in school. I'm not as adorably pathetic anymore. Now me and Dad, we're just a couple of pathetic guys; no longer a sorry man and his unfortunate son.

A bum walks toward me with his eyes on the bag near Dad's head. I haven't eaten in two days. The bum probably hasn't eaten in weeks. He smells of booze. At least Dad isn't a bum because he's addicted to alcohol. He's just stupid.

'Hey, darling,' the bum says when he gets closer. I'm curled up around my knees and my hair covers most of my face. I might look female to him. 'Say, how about we have a feast?' He veers toward Dad.

'You can't take it,' I say. My voice is high.

The bum turns back to me, staggering. 'You're a pretty thing,' he says. 'You could be a girl.'

I go to stand, but the bum stops me with his hand on my head. He pushes my hair back from my face and leans down to look at me. His breath reeks of alcohol and rot.

He pulls my head up, and my scalp hurts again. My arm hangs limp and bruised at my side. I try to push away the hand in my hair, but with only one good arm I can't do much. The bum wheezes a laugh, and then slides his free hand into his pants.

'You're small, but I think you can open your mouth wide, yeah?' His hand jerks a few times in his pants, shallow and quick.

'Let me go.' I hope Dad will hear me. I can hear him snoring behind me.

The bum pulls his pants down with one hand and jerks my head up hard. His pubic hair is as filthy and matted as the hair on his head. His crotch smells worse than his breath. I'm eye level to his belly button. I try not to look down.

'Open up,' the bum says, pulling hard on my hair. My eyes sting, but I keep my mouth shut.

The bum is too loud. Dad snores. The bum looks down at me. The sleeping bag rustles like Dad is moving in his sleep. The bum grabs my nose and holds it closed. Keeping my mouth closed makes me choke on air. It's better than the alternative. And Dad will be here soon.

My lungs hurt. The bum doesn't let his grip go. He pulls my hair as he falls to the side. Dad stands over the bum. He doesn't look at me. He steps on the bum's neck with his broken shoe.

'Check his pockets,' Dad says.

I search through dirty pockets. I find a half-empty bottle of alcohol in the first pocket. In the second pocket there's a knife. I hand the knife to Dad.

'Nice knife,' he says to the bum. 'The kind that's good for killing men who try to fuck with my son.'

I could sneak over and grab one of the burritos now. But my head hurts and my arm hurts and Dad is acting weird, so I stay.

'Just kidding—' the bum gasps under Dad's foot.

'Not funny,' Dad says. He steps harder on the bum's neck.

The bum tries to move, but he can't. His pants are still pulled down. His face turns red and then purple before Dad lets off some of the pressure.

'Tell you what,' Dad says. 'I'll give you a head start. If I can still see you in ten seconds, I'll fucking kill you.' He takes his foot off the bum's neck and steps back.

The bum scrambles to stand up as Dad stares him down and starts to count.

'One,' he says, all quiet and serious.

When Dad's at seven, the bum turns the corner and is out of sight. Dad yells after him, 'Stay the fuck away!'

'You okay, Jay?' Dad kneels next to me, pushing my head up with a hand under my chin. He rubs a hand over my head and lets the weight of it rest on the back of my neck.

I don't cry. Dad taught me not to cry years ago. But he sees something in my eyes.

'I got you,' he says. He pushes his dirty forehead against mine; his hair falls into my face and some gets in my mouth. It's gross, but I don't move. I push back with my forehead. For a moment, I feel warm.

Dad says it again and again.

'I got you.'

BIRDFEED
Emma Phillips

MUM is a bird.

Some say she's fragile but she always says we are who we are and she's a bird for sure. One time Dad brought a Chinese calendar from the takeaway so I checked and she was born in the year of the rooster. It said I'm a rabbit, and Dad is a horse.

Dad likes birds. Years back, they kept budgies but they had to give them away when I was born; their carry-on woke me up. 'Bit cruel', Mum had said, 'keeping them in cages like that. Drove me mad, you know, the way they used to imitate.' *They recognised their own*, I thought but didn't say.

Mum is small, like a canary. On good days she wears greens and yellows to show off her hair and smooth skin. She uses her bird voice to sing around the kitchen and, when she hits the high notes, she can really warble. 'Your Mum's pretty', the kids at school say when she turns up to get me.

They signed the piece of paper to say I can walk home on my own, which I mostly do. But when Mum feels like preening she'll come in. I see people notice her first then look at me as if to say, are you sure you belong together? Dad is plain too but Mum says the lookers break your heart and by the time he came along she wanted someone she could rely on. Birds need a lot of looking after, you see. Especially when somebody ruffles their feathers. Then we all lie low.

Mum has a lot of what you might call temporary jobs. She's a part timer, really, on account of her feathers. When she starts a new job, she'll be all chirpy but offices are never the right habitat so it's only a matter of time before things get heated. The squawking and name calling start and no amount of closed doors and hushed phone calls can disguise the fact that there'll be another migration. Birds have to migrate for survival.

When I was really small I used to migrate too. But then Gran put her foot down and told Mum it wasn't fair to change my school again. She said Mum had to start trying to get on with people. So Dad deals with most of the school stuff, and Mum makes contact on the days she feels like roosting.

Dad had the same job for ages but lately he's changed, so I walk myself to school in the mornings because he has to leave earlier. He gets more money and at first I didn't mind. I got a pocket money rise and he'd bring Mum these little presents, but now I wish he was there by half past five, like he used to. Especially on the days when Mum is nocturnal. Then I hardly see her because she only gets up when it's dark and the rest of the time she's in bed, all puffed up with the curtains drawn. When Mum's nocturnal, she smells funny.

She's usually up by the time Dad gets home, which is always after dark, but she hardly ever gets dressed anymore. Before he got the new job Dad would cook, and on Fridays we'd have takeaway. In any case, we kept Mum out of the kitchen to avoid the squawking. Birds find it tricky to follow instructions so recipes are out of the question and Mum has, in her own words, 'zero interest in cooking.' She says that in this day and age women are beyond that gender crap. That means Dad did it until he got the new job, and a lady called Sylvia comes in twice a week to help with the cleaning. Except Mum doesn't think she does it right. So Sylvia hasn't been for a while and I think Dad might have to go down to the newsagents again like he did when Joan stopped coming.

Since Dad got his job he doesn't have time to cook anymore, so he mostly gets us dinner in boxes. He still does mine first but I wish he'd do Mum's. Then I could sit and talk to him instead of watching TV while he gets theirs ready. A big plate for Dad who eats a lot like me but a side plate for Mum because birds have smaller appetites. She says it's healthier to eat little and often but Gran says that's nonsense for children. Once, it made them argue.

I don't really like it when Mum is nocturnal. At school, we did a project on animals that sleep in the daytime but unless Mum sleeps with her eyes open she's not doing it right. I know we're all different but I prefer it when she is diurnal like me. I like big words. My teachers say I've got an ear for language. On parents' evening, Mum puffs her chest out and calls me her little dictionary. She says it just loud enough for other parents to hear. Then I feel proud, especially when the Dads start looking at her. Dads like Mum a lot. One even winked at her when Dad wasn't looking. They were getting on well then. After parents' evening, we went to the pub for dinner. Mum had a white wine spritzer and she sat there laughing at Dad's jokes, even the ones he always tells that aren't very funny. We stayed so long I had pudding twice, loads of Coke, and missed my bedtime. I didn't care though. I would've stayed forever.

That's the last time I heard Mum laugh. Her real laugh, not the shrill one she uses when Gran tells her stories or the strange empty one she did on the phone once when Dad called to say he wasn't coming home. The other two are bird laughs. When I can't sleep, I think about the pub night and try to work out what I might have done wrong. Even when I got top marks for spelling and they put my name in the newsletter, we didn't do anything to celebrate, not even chips.

Mum is supposed to be doing dinner for me now so I can eat earlier, but when she's nocturnal I know better than to ask. She only cocks her head and looks at me funny. I don't go up there much.

When Dad gets angry, which hardly ever happens, he calls her Alison in a cross voice. One time, when I was meant to be downstairs, he got angry and I heard everything. He said she was selfish and irresponsible. The funny thing was she never said anything. Probably just sat there, staring at him and looking ambushed. Birds are very sensitive.

Now I have school dinners and stuff from the boxes and once a week I go to Gran's for tea. We eat fish fingers off trays we put our plates on to keep our laps clean and if you pick your plate up there's a picture of this lady who was Prince William and Prince Harry's Mum. Gran says she was killed in an accident in Paris before I was born. Mum says Gran hasn't told me the half of it and one day she and I will sit down and have a proper chat about the monarchy. That's the thing about Mum, she really knows stuff. Birds are cleverer than humans in a lot of ways.

I saw this programme about how birds can sense storms coming, so they circle the tree tops, calling and warning each other. Maybe Mum knew the letdown was coming, which was why she stayed perched in her room for so long. She probably didn't fancy getting her feathers wet. That's what she called it, the letdown. 'Your Dad has let us down.' I knew something odd was going on when I came home and saw Gran's shoes on the step. It was a Wednesday and Gran only ever comes over on Sundays to pick me up—so Mum and Dad can have a bit of time to themselves.

I wonder if Mum will need time to herself now Dad has let us down, and I feel a bit scared in case she stays nocturnal. Gran is looking at me with her worried face, the one she used when I had my appendix out. I'm looking at Mum, thinking how skinny she is, and Mum has curled her feet over and isn't looking at anyone. She's gripping the bottom of her dressing gown between her toes so tightly she seems to find it hard to stay upright. So I decide to act like it doesn't matter even though I feel like I do when I stand on my head for too long and the blood flows backwards.

What I'm really wondering is, what are we going to do? Gran offers to move in for a bit. I say 'yes' but Mum says 'no'. I don't want to knock her off balance so I quickly change my answer.

'No, we'll be fine and we'll see you on Sunday.' I say, and Mum looks at me gratefully. I'd like to crawl into her lap but in this family we roost sitting up. Then she goes nocturnal.

A house can feel empty when someone is there. *Inappropriate responsibility*, they call it. Later, Mum squawks louder than ever, cursing Dad's name to anyone who'll listen while I warm our dinner from one of the boxes. She pecks at the plate the way she tells me not to. She has a drink then and her words get sloppy. I go to bed and shut her out with a pillow. When I wake up, I can hear her crying so I dig my nails into my palms and wish I had claws.

The next day, she tells me never to mention Dad again and I agree, but I've got my fingers crossed so it won't count! Every night, before I sleep, I pray to the God she doesn't believe in. 'Heavenly Father,' I say, 'Help us out.' But I don't think he is listening.

Mum is getting thinner and refuses the toast I am living on. I learn a lot about bird food and I think the letdown is really a disappearance. Again, Gran offers to move in but Mum says there's no room and when Gran says it's hardly a case of Bethlehem, they shout. Gran says I can stay with her while Mum sorts herself out but I say no. Mum tells her that we're coping.

It's a hard winter and I hear on the news that bird behaviour is changing so I look for signs. They say I've been bottling things up but what they don't know is that I'm preparing. While Mum has been fluffing up to keep warm, I've been working on my hummingbird technique.

Birds can drop their body temperature at night to conserve oxygen. It helps them survive the winter. In hummingbirds, this is called torpor. I am part bird. Mum is still nocturnal. I go to school and when I feel angry, I try camouflage. Some birds lay speckled eggs to put off hunters. It helps them blend in the nest. I wish I could stay home and practise. If I could be camouflaged, I might not need to think.

I have to remember the birdfeed. When I get home, I make something to eat. I look in the cupboards and find some crusts, which I dip into jam. There's a sweet at the bottom of my bag so I put it on the plate for good measure. I take it up the stairs but my feet get heavy. It doesn't seem like a surprise anymore. When I get to the top it's quiet, but I haven't been back very long so it's early.

'Wake up, Mum!' I call from the doorway. There's silence except for my breathing. I push the door open and she has gone.

Vamoose. She doesn't leave feathers.

THE SECOND COMING
Cath Barton

'So what are you offering me?' I said.

'Sweets. Lovely homemade sweets,' was the sandy-haired man's reply.

It's not common these days to have people knocking at your door trying to sell you things. Time was there'd be the Encyclopaedia Britannica man. Well, so people said, I never met one myself. I always thought you'd have to be pretty desperate to take a job like that. You could go for weeks without selling a single copy, so when you met that rare person who was in need of an encyclopaedia and willing to buy it from you, it must have been a cause for a celebration. Half a lager and lime and a packet of crisps down at The Cat and Dragon.

Sweets of course, even lovely homemade ones, are at the opposite extreme. Low cost, high volume, isn't that the expression? And they did look nice, so I bought a quarter of Sandy's peppermint creams. He had them all measured out in the smart red satchel slung over his shoulder, and he pulled out a little white paper bag and thrust it towards me, an eager smile on his thin lips. 'Anything else?' he asked.

A picture flashed into my mind of the sweetie shop I used to go to when I was eight years old. On a Saturday morning, with my pocket money hot in my hand. There they all were before me: fruit chews, liquorice laces, sherbet fountains, coconut mushrooms and those flying saucers that I didn't care for because the outside tasted like cardboard. Oh, and gobstoppers. Just the thought and I could taste them rolling in my mouth.

'Have you got any sherbet lemons?' I heard myself saying.

'No, sorry, we don't do those,' he said, his voice drooping.

'They used to be my favourites.'

'Mine too, but I can't get them right.'

What could I do? I know you're not supposed to invite strange men into your house, but this was different. We shared a love of sherbet lemons. He couldn't be a rapist or a murderer.

I made tea and when I carried it through to the living room—proper cups and saucers, and a tray cloth—Sandy was sitting on a hard chair, his knees firmly jammed together.

'Do sit somewhere more comfortable,' I said as I put the tray down on the Isle of Wight-shaped coffee table.

'I'm okay,' he said. 'I was just admiring your table. I went there once.'

'Did you get one of those glass test-tubes filled with layers of different coloured sands from Alum Bay?' I asked, remembering the disappointment at how quickly mine had got shaken up, muddying all the once-bright colours.

Sandy told me all about the holiday he'd had on the Island when he was a boy. I wondered whether we might have been there at the same time. Stood next to one another looking at the Alum Bay cliffs maybe. I often do that—wonder whether I've passed someone in the street without knowing that in the future, in another town or country, we would be friends or lovers.

'Someone wrote that the past is another country, didn't they?'

'Sorry?'

I'd startled Sandy, dragged him back from some memory. His eyes had darkened.

'It doesn't matter,' I said, over-brightly. 'Tell me about your business. How did you get into making sweeties?'

But I wasn't really interested in his business. I wasn't interested in this door-to-door salesman. I hadn't even asked him his name. Sherbet lemons and Alum Bay sands were in the past and I wanted him to go. After a few more desultory exchanges, he slurped the dregs of his tea and I shuddered. I couldn't help myself.

He cleared his throat to speak again, but before he could start there was a loud rap at the front door. I jumped up, glad of the interruption.

On the doorstep stood the same sandy-haired man. Just like the first time he asked if I could spare a couple of minutes, that he wouldn't detain me for long but that I would most certainly want to hear what he had to say. He had the same smart red satchel, the same thin lips, the same eager smile. I heard the same words coming out of my mouth.

'So what are you offering me?'

And I knew what his reply would be. And that, this time, there would be no sweeties in the satchel.

A GALILEAN QUARTET
Abigail Wyatt

i.

I scarcely recall how it all came about. Perhaps it was girlish excitement. If it was my idea I have forgotten now, but I cannot believe that it was. What I do remember is the throbbing of the drums and the power of the music. It raised me up and bore me along, as weightless as a spar in a flood. I allowed it to break over me, wave after wave, and it bathed my limbs and my torso. It was as if my spirit dipped and dived in a shining, singing sea.

Afterwards, when the instruments ceased, there was a moment of pure, ringing silence. Then the applause broke over my head as though I were a rock on the shore. I felt his eyes all over me, of course, and I saw how the sweat stained his tunic. His slack mouth hung open and his tongue slavered and lolled.

It was not that I thought to rouse his appetites. I wanted him to know he couldn't have me. When I bowed my head my hair fell down, and I used it like a veil. As I lay there panting, I felt nothing much but the triumph of my own grace and power. Power, they say, is an aphrodisiac, and it's true that I liked it best of all.

ii.

There was a lot of nasty gossip at the time, but the damage was none of my doing. She threw herself at him, a bitch on heat, over and over again. I didn't want to see it at first. I tried to make excuses. But, after she simpered and cooed like a child, she set herself to writhing like a whore. Still, on that particular evening, she seemed to take leave of her senses. She whirled and twisted and fell at his feet like some pox-ridden harlot from the quay. It's hard for me to say this—after all, I am her mother—but the creature has no heart and no pride, and certainly no loyalty. After everything I did for her, to have treated me like this.

Not that I'm saying he didn't egg her on. He did—but he did it just to spite me. He looked on *her* to humble *me*. He said I was too wilful and too proud. But wasn't it for love of *him* that *I* braved the anger of my people? Was I wilful and proud and in need of being 'humbled' when first he thought to take me to his bed? And, though he was king, and though it was his feast, am I not his wife and his consort? And yet a vain and silly child made fools of us both.

Worse than that, he exposed us to both ridicule and danger. She sashayed her pretty little tush and played him like a catfish on a pole. Afterwards, in the market place, there were scurrilous verses and much laughter. And always, in the palace, there were those who waited and watched.

I tried to make light of it. I turned the other cheek.

'What care I,' I said to them, 'for the fate of a wandering madman?'

But people believe what they *want* to believe. It happens so often in politics: an uncia of rumour is worth an as of fact.

iii.

It was a sad affair. I'll grant you that, and I do feel partly responsible. On the other hand, I wouldn't want you thinking that I acted out of malice. If I'd seen which way the wind was blowing, I might have been a little more prudent. I liked the man, for God's sake; you might even say I admired him. He was big and burly with the strength of a lion and eyes that burned deep into your soul. He talked well, too. He wasn't glib or slick—sometimes he was downright coarse—but you only had to look at him to see that he meant what he said. It was funny how he made you *believe* in him. It was a trick *I* could have done with. He had a way of putting things simply and getting directly to the point.

It was no wonder that the priests were afraid of him. He could outsmart them at their own game. And I admit, too, that I was nervous. The whole situation was unstable. But quite what the girl had against him, I still don't know for sure. There was talk she'd tipped her cap at him, but surely that was just kitchen gossip. And, anyway, why would she cast her eyes on a character like him?

But then you have to ask yourself: why *did* she do it? Her body, it's true, was sweet as a peach but her mind was stony ground. If you want my opinion, the genius behind it was that sharp-nosed shrew of a mother. Now there was a woman who knows her own business—and everyone else's as well. For my part, though, I'll admit I spoke rashly. Later, I lived to regret it. Where was my alternative? I had already given my word.

iv.

I was despatched that very night and arrived there early the next morning. The first pale blush of dawn was pinking up the sky. There was no standing on ceremony. It was straight down to business. The officer of the watch was careful to double check my orders. He sucked in air through his rotting teeth and would not meet my eye.

'Rather you than me,' he said. 'I've yet to break my fast this morning. I'll summon an escort by and by, and find you a sack or two.'

After he left, I drew my sword and tried its blade with my finger. When they pushed open the creaking door, The Baptist was already on his knees.

CRISIS OF PERSONALITY
Miki Byrne

IN my previous life I was a rabbit. I puzzle over how I know I was a rabbit. I suspect that when I was hit—crossing the A38 outside Kings Coughton in the Midlands—something went askew. I suspect the speed with which I catapulted from that life to this one was so great that part of the transition knocked the normal procedure out of kilter. It has left me in a very peculiar situation.

I often dream that I am a rabbit. Powerful vivid dreams in which I am small, hiding under a hedgerow, or lolloping across a meadow. I frequently feel an incredible desire to be outside; to crawl under great stands of bracken or to lie quietly beneath clumps of buttercups. I get an almost visceral kick from the smell of grass and leaves and feel the need to run when I hear a harvester growling over the fields near my home.

Salad is always my favourite food.

Sometimes I lie in bed at night longing for the land, but I am confined indoors: too warm, too constricted. In summer I creep out to sleep in the garden.

I feel the urge to wash long ears and whiskers that aren't there. It must be similar to the phantom limb feeling that amputees experience.

When I am upset, I develop a twitch in my nose and an urge to thump the floor with my foot, as if to warn the others in my colony. The fact that I have neighbours instead is irrelevant.

I hate being tall. I would rather be close to the pungent growing earth than towering over paved streets and acres of tarmac.

When I'm in a supermarket, I spend hours in the fruit and vegetable aisles. I was once caught shoplifting. Thankfully, when he saw I had only taken three bags of carrots, the manager just thought I was loopy and decided not to prosecute. He gave me the same look that my dentist did when I refused correctional braces for my lovely long front teeth. I have been very careful since then. I decided to grow some things of my own. It's much safer and more convenient. Mind you, in winter I have no choice but to shop. I have to exercise enormous self-discipline.

The worst thing though is the pull that the land has over me. I walk the fields for hours. I come home exhausted and feel lost, rootless. I am attempting to dig out my own burrow in the back garden. So that I can smell the earth all around me and see the tiny little roots that suspend from the roof of my earth cave. I want to see the shiny skin of worms close up, and become re-acquainted with all the little crawly things that are such good company. I'm not skilled in construction though and digging as a human is much harder and more complicated than simply using my claws and instinct.

I have to hide my construction under the shed. The neighbours would think I'm mad. I suppose they wouldn't be far wrong but I can't help it. The pull is too strong. I've thought of seeking help. Maybe a doctor or psychiatrist could put me right but I don't want to be any different. If I regress further, become broody for loads of children or develop a huge sexual appetite, then I'm sure somebody will notice and come to my rescue, bringing the requisite sedative and smooth-voiced therapist. Until then I'll just carry on being a burrow-maker and land-lover.

By the way, since we are getting to know each other, my name is Bernadette—but my friends call me Bunny.

Free To Loving Home
(Donation Required)
Michelle Ann King

'Good morning, everyone! Welcome to the Hugh Everett Rehoming Centre. My name is Hendrik and I'll be your facilitator today. Firstly, I'd like to thank you all for coming. I know that interdimensional travel is time-consuming, physically debilitating and, for some of you, illegal. It can also be rather disconcerting to meet your alternates, so we do have counsellors available on site for advice and support—although I am obliged to point out that attendance is at your own risk and the Centre cannot accept liability for any loss, damage, personal injury or emotional distress caused during your visit.

But that's enough about the small print! I'm sure that when you meet Paul, you'll agree that this superb opportunity was well worth the effort.

As advised in your initial query packs, this version of Paul is 33 years old and was rescued from a continuum in which human society was destroyed due to a viral pandemic. However, I can reassure you that Paul has been extensively tested and confirmed to be genetically immune to both the host-world virus and all current notifiable contagions. Furthermore, we provide an enhanced immunisation package specifically tailored to the successful application.

Now, you'll notice that Paul is currently a little underweight and showing some signs of...well, shall we say wear and tear? This is to be expected given the hardships and privations endured in his prior living conditions. He hasn't had it easy this last year, poor guy! So he's not exactly looking his best right now, but apart from the dermal scarring and some decreased liver function due to a period of alcohol misuse, he is in perfectly fine physical health. We expect the leg to heal completely, and—with a balanced diet, sober living and access to medical care—he has a projected life expectancy of another thirty-seven years, so I think you'll all agree that's still tremendous value for money!

I do also need to make you aware of the possibility that there could be some psychological damage that won't become evident until Paul is resettled. Our Behavioural Advice Line will be available to you free of charge for three months, although you will be required to sign a disclaimer releasing the Centre from all responsibility. Even if you don't have relevant treatment facilities in your home worlds, some good old fashioned love and affection can do wonders, am I right? Of course, I am!

In this Paul's personal history, both parents were killed in a road accident when he was 23 so, mums and dads, you'll need to allow for that developmental gap in re-establishing your relationship. But, I'm sure you'll all agree, he grew up into a fine young man! And obviously, he'll be thrilled with any of you.

Ma'am, are you all right? Would you like some water? We can take a break, no? Right, I'll continue.

Before the breakdown of his society, Paul was employed in the field of law enforcement. While I appreciate that might not be a viable option in all potential destinations, it's still evidence of valuable training, skills and experience that will be an asset to any dimension. Paul married at 25 and divorced at 30, after his Megan had an affair. Megans, please bear that in mind—even if you are one of the ones who stayed faithful, this Paul will come with trust issues you'll need to work through. Lynettes, I'm sorry; his timeline played out differently, he won't know you. That's not to say, however, that he won't learn to love you just the way yours did. We all understand that no marriage comes with a guarantee of success, but your previous history means you'll certainly have a head start with this one!

Okay then, unless you have any questions we will open the floor to bidding. Remember, the charitable donations of our patrons is what keeps this facility going and allows us to provide rescue and rehabilitation for people like Paul, and second chances for all who loved him. Oh, and while we're running your credit checks there will be refreshments served in the reception room. Thank you for your attention, ladies and gentlemen, and good luck!'

THE CROWNING
Jay R Thurston

THE mature ones stood over twice my height. Simple minds in oversized craniums. I folded my arms and waited for the crouched yellow-headed female to cease stroking my hair with her grooming implement.

'Such a little doll, Megan. You're gonna knock 'em dead.' She beamed a proud smile.

Don't tempt me, Mother.

Other shortlings and their adult caretakers scurried about, leading the taller beings here and there, pouts and tantrums abundant. Over Mother's shoulder, the only familiar person my height read a newspaper while her matron equivalent fluffed her red locks.

'Can I talk to Paige?' I asked Mother.

'How about we get you dressed first, dear? The pageant is starting soon.'

'I want to talk to Paige!' I demanded.

'No need to take that tone, Megan.'

Whatever. I stomped away before she could finish, grabbed Paige's hand, and dragged her to a side room. A row of well-lit make-up stations took up the far wall. A collection of staff tended to a brunette shortling in the corner, powdering her face, rolling her hair, sliding a cherry-coloured dress over her head. The commotion provided enough privacy.

Paige's eyes remained on the newspaper.

'Master Vage, this isn't what we thought it to be,' I said.

'Look here,' she spoke. 'They found Bidifir. They call it Kepler 22b. What kind of a name is that?'

'They have? Should we fear an attack?'

'Hah! They can hardly see it with their technology, never mind get there, look!' She spun the newspaper. A blue and white marble floated against a speckled black backdrop. The picture was terrible quality, but it was enough.

Our home city, Dargan, was located on the unseen side of the planet. Ah, the clean air, the cool nights, the home cooked food—I could practically taste the roasted sea turkey with winter apple glaze and side of camel turnips and tundra wheat. Every backwards planet we've since claimed has lacked any amenities quite like home. And their technologies were crude and laughable at best!

Paige's voice returned me to reality. 'What's your concern, Teggan?'

'I think our forms have been misinterpreted.'

'Nonsense,' the girl's chubby cheeks dimpled as she smiled. 'I did my homework. The stray transmission we picked up gave all the info required. We're right where we want to be. We're practically worshipped.'

'The tall ones seem a bit patronizing.'

'Teggan,' Master Vage pointed to the four year old at the make-up station. 'Look at that shortling. Six servants for her. *Six.* I'm telling you, we're in control.

'Jelly beans!' The brunette girl wailed. A servant scampered away to her demand.

I wasn't one to question his judgment. He's the mastermind. I'm Lieutenant Teggan, his oath-sworn bodyguard, hand chosen by the High Empress of Bidifir as the best possible warrior available to Vage's service, and if necessary, disposal. He did the thinking, I protected and followed orders. This planet was not our first, nor our toughest victim. We've roused rebellions, fought entire militaries, and kidnapped top officials. This Earth should be child's play. Literally. But something just wasn't right.

'What are the plans, Master Vage?' I asked.

'Stop calling me that. Call me by my shortling alias.'

'Master Paige—'

'Just Paige.'

Sigh. Always in character. 'When will we make our move?'

The door opened. Both mothers entered, each toting a small dress in a clear bag.

'There you are,' Mother blurted. 'It's time to get you dressed and ready!'

'We'll talk later,' Paige said.

'Why not now?' I argued.

The women propped us into side-by-side make-up stations, and set up various coloured tools on the vanity.

Paige answered, 'Just play along.'

Just play along. Pssh. 'They're not going to remember, anyway.'

'I'd rather not mind wipe them here.'

'We made these women believe we're their daughters. We've implanted four years of false memories. I don't think scrubbing a couple minutes of conversation is a big deal.'

Mother removed my tank top and for a moment I swam within powder blue fabric until my arms found the puffy sleeves. With my long and obnoxious hair brushed forward over my shoulders, Mother buttoned the dress up my back. I looked at Paige. She was wearing a similar dress in mint-green.

'*Megan,*' Paige stressed my shortling name. 'This pageant they refer to is a crowning ceremony. Once one of us is crowned, we'll acquire more servants. It's the first step towards taking charge of this punitive planet.'

'Are you sure?'

'The stray transmission told me so. The Earthlings broadcast these events on their mass media. They will follow our every order without the slightest resistance.'

'Shouldn't we have assumed larger forms? Aren't we at a disadvantage fighting as shortlings?'

'Who said anything about fighting them?'

I frowned. Master Vage's calculated plans kept my combat prowess in reserve more often than I liked.

'We want to keep as many of them as intact as we can,' Vage continued in his squeaky voice. 'We don't want another incident like Bolian Four.'

How could I forget? The pandemic that spread after our arrival on Bolian Four completely destroyed the population. They had no immunity to the germs we brought. We needed not spill any blood. A boring victory. At least we still claimed resources for Bidifir, although the High Empress was unhappy at the loss of labour force. Since then, we've undergone tedious decontamination protocol and taken the forms of indigenous beings when arriving on a new planet.

'Jelly beans!' Paige yelled in her mother's face; the woman dismissed herself immediately.

'What are jelly beans?' I asked.

'Don't know, but if the shortling over there requested them, it's important to assimilate.'

Always thinking, that Master Paige. A powder puffer to the face left my vision clouded.

'This planet is hostile enough. We'll overtake them peacefully, with charm.' Paige wore a dastardly expression on her cherubic face. Conquest by charm. It was certainly unconventional. By this point in most adventures, Vage would've tasked me with carrying out an assassination plot, or cutting off a vital resource. This adventure involved getting my eyelids plastered by a strange Earthling that thinks I'm her precious little Megan.

Paige's mother returned with a colourful selection in a plastic bowl. She placed the bowl on the chiffon across Paige's lap and resumed grooming her mane.

'Hmm, not bad,' Paige popped jelly beans into her mouth.

Mother grabbed my cheeks and drew on my lips with a smeary stick. Unable to talk, I listened.

'The Earthlings have not only located but have roused interest in our planet, Teggan. It's imperative we monitor their next move.'

Mother stopped me from nodding. 'Stay still, dear.'

Paige continued, 'We will assume reign methodically and in good time. An aggressive strike so close to their discovery of Bidifir would be brash. No need to get them worried. Worry leads to overreactions, and we've still got a lot of recon to do before we get them running around on high alert.'

I gazed into the unconditional, loving eyes of the Earth woman pulling at my lashes; the stare a pet would offer its owner. So brainwashed.

Paige's mother motioned to apply make-up, causing Paige to shriek, 'Back off, woman!'

Master Vage has the tantrums down, although I hadn't heard any other shortling call her mother *woman*, but who was I to judge? My lips now glossy to Mother's satisfaction, I spoke freely. 'If you are confident we can take the planet by these means, I follow your command.'

Paige spoke through inflated cheeks and stained teeth, 'I've been thinking about it. I want you to take the crown in this pageant.'

'Me?'

'With you as the figurehead, I'll be allowed to continue my recon without having the spotlight on me. You're the decoy.'

'Our girls talk about the strangest things,' Paige's mother said to mine as she draped a wide ribbon across Paige's dress.

'Hit them,' Paige demanded.

I focused into each of their eyes in turn. With a light burst from mine, their memories of the last minutes were cleared.

A male voice announced from the door, 'Pageant's about to start, girls to the stage.'

'Ooh, we almost forgot your shoes!' Both mothers rushed to our feet as if nothing unusual had happened. I glanced at Paige. This wasn't so bad, being treated like royalty.

Paige issued instructions in a hushed tone. 'Wave and smile like you're the High Empress and they, your underlings.'

Flaunt dominance? Hardly a stretch. Even the strongest Earthlings would not stand a chance against my natural form. Wave and smile while Master Vage brainwashed them into crowning me. Child's play.

'Yes Mast—I mean, Paige.'

Our mothers lifted us from our thrones, tugged at our dresses and fussed over the finishing touches.

'Ladies and gentlemen, thank you for coming to the Miss Kentucky Sweetheart Pageant!' The male voice spoke again through the intercom.

Mother held my hand and escorted me from the room.

Paige insisted on being carried.

As my flats slid across the rug in the hall, I revelled in the plan. If Vage wanted to put me in charge, so be it. I would wear the coveted tiara and rule the pageant. He'd remain occupied with all the footwork while I'd amass the servants to an army, and oust crowned girls from other territories. Yes, I could grow to like this. Starting with Kentucky, this world would be ours.

My sneer of glee went unmet. Paige mimicked another shortling, sucking her opposable digit.

Ours? Scratch that.

Mine.

I Have God to Thank for Everything

Barry Pomeroy

PRAISE Jesus that He has given me the strength to go on when so many others have succumbed. I do not pretend to know what His will is for me, but I willingly submit to His plan. As long as I can, I will wait for a sign from Him.

There were many, such as the machine people for instance, who rejected God in the final days of the plague. As we know from scripture, such action is more than medical error. God doles out health and sickness where He wills, and woe be unto him who questions God's ways or rejects Him.

Luckily I was brought up to love God and to protect His word. Due to God's forbearance I am still here, eking out an existence to His glory while so many others are gone.

The machine people were the first casualties. They gave their machine explanation to the plague God had loosed upon the world. They said an ordinary virus—since when is any representation of His will *ordinary?*—had mutated and become fatal.

Because of their wickedness and their rejection of God (although I too am a sinner and in no position to judge) they were the first to die. Bodies were left choking in the rivers and in almost all the public water supplies. Since one of the effects of the virus was dehydration, sufferers felt the burning of hell so they would know what they were going to encounter for eternity.

God didn't just take the sinners, of course. He chose that moment to call home many of the righteous, my parents amongst them. Holy people who gave their lives to spreading His word, who brought their children up in the light of Jesus, instead of the pale illumination of the machine people's electricity. There were many who questioned their decision to bring their children to the Lord. I was fourteen and a prophet of Jesus when the machine people, in their mistaken sinner way, came to take my sister and brothers away.

They claimed that the devoutness of our parents, the strictness of their holy teachings, was abuse, and they kept my younger siblings.

They sent them to school and reworked their minds until even my sister, who was eleven when she was taken from truth, could barely be recognized. She came back to us eventually, when she was sixteen, but five years of being led into wickedness and sin had taken a toll on her.

Her ways were disrespectful and wanton. She cut her hair and wore machine people clothes, instead of the honest garb of our faith. She talked to boys and, some said, to men. When she left us it was no surprise. No one blamed my parents for first trying to exorcise her demons before casting her out; she had fallen from Jesus' way and was no longer fit company.

My other siblings, I never saw again. They became mere scions of the machine people. Living in the tall buildings in the city, rubbing elbows with thousands of others, they lost track of their humble supplication before the divine, and became minions of Satan.

After my sister's exorcism, my parents were taken from me for a time. The machine people, in their infinitely interfering ways, put their mere laws of the flesh above those of holiness. They charged my devout parents with attempted murder. My sister, who had become more of a machine person than we thought, spoke against our family from her hospital bed, condemned our parents and brought them low before the injustice of sinners.

When my parents returned to me—an outcome I expedited by praying at least three hours every day—they came back with a plan. They had seen many evil things in the machine people's city. *It was worse than they thought*, they told me. So they asked me to study.

I had no direction at first, but then I felt the Lord's hand guiding me through the texts, helping me to discard the information that was of no use. My weak mortal head became packed with uneasy ideas, for the books were written by sinners.

The misguided machine people provided our colony with thousands of books, which we used for fires in the winter storms. The supply was nearly endless. They wantonly went from idea to idea, since they weren't blessed with the fixity of attention that God could give them.

When I first began to read the books, some people in our community spoke against it and recalled to us my sister's flagrant ways. I was presented to them, stripped to the service of our lord although the way to the meeting hall was dark and cold in the winter. There, I presented myself and submitted my will to God. I told them of my holy path, which can only lead to righteousness; God's hand was in mine, and they bowed before His will.

While I studied, the world changed around us. My siblings were sent to convince us to leave the asceticism of our community and to join the machine people. I was not alone in denouncing them, and sending them weeping back to their cold machines. Here, we want for nothing. We have God to thank for the land which provides us with food, and the rain that gives us water to drink, and the houses He has directed us to build. We have God to thank for the endless supplies of books that keep us warm. We want for nothing.

When the cold winter was sent to test us, some succumbed; their eagerness to join the Lord was more powerful than the wish to stay with the mortals and tend our souls. We didn't envy them their joy. We would humbly receive our own reward once our work was done. The machine people were outraged though, when they discovered that half of our tiny colony had crept away in the night to be with the Lord. Likely, they saw it as desertion; for they had set themselves up before God on the bare earth, little realizing that the sin of pride goeth before a fall.

They came to our colony with their transport machines and endeavoured to force us to leave. While they stood in the snow, in their machine clothing that heated them artificially, I was amongst the righteous who, removing our clothes, called upon their materialistic world to smite us. I stood praising Jesus, invulnerable to the gnawing cold, while snow settled on the transports of the machine people. Seeing my example, and that of others to whom the Lord had given strength, the machine people left, although they took what was most precious to us. They took our children.

In the meeting hall, amidst supplication before God and anguish that our future had been taken away from us, my intent was finally revealed to our people. They needed hope in their dark moment, and the

Lord decided that my studies were to be that hope. I told them that my path lay as a shining river before me and in a few years, if God chose to let me continue, we would achieve our goal. I still remember the crying upon God for his mercy and the sudden gleam of hope in their eyes. I was suddenly elevated to a direct servant of God, although I hastened to tell them that all were putty in His hands and that if we do His will, our works cannot help but be good.

Once their solace was achieved, as much as that was possible in those trying times, I turned to my studies with redoubled force. God gave me the strength to read night and day, and Jesus' holy finger sometimes limned the page ahead of my tired eyes, divulging the most fruitful path. My studiousness even came to the attention of the machine people, which I realise now was the Lord's will. By whispering in their ears the area of my study, and keeping the intent silent, God ensured that they participated in their own salvation. How present His will in all our doings. How glory-filled is His every wish.

The machine people, once God had so directed them, bought me equipment for a lab. They were delighted, in their childlike way, that one of us from the colony would take an interest in their science.

Although they said nothing, we could see they intended to drive a wedge between us and the holy way we had chosen. Without children to influence, however, their equipment meant nothing to our community. I worked ceaselessly though the spring nights and into the next winter, until I had achieved my goal.

I won't say that I wasn't tempted, like any mortal, by the invites of the machine people. I looked away from their scanty clothes when their women came to act the part of men in the setting up of equipment, but I could not help the roving of my sinner thoughts. I held my mind to task, knowing that I was a tool in the hand of God, who was pushing me to excel, and pulling all of us into a glorious future.

Our community suffered the attention of the machine people. Some came to peer at our lives, like mere tourists, and exclaimed that we lived in *shacks*, as they called them, without the benefits of the modern world.

Many of our number stood up to them and explained how God is the only benefit of the world; living in all time as He does, He is the most modern of conveniences.

They laughed in our faces, almost helplessly, as we explained the rapture and the four riders. They spoke against the soul, as if the body were not mere meat moving through the glory of the Lord, and said instead that we were acids that break down when we die.

Luckily, for the faith of our community, I had been studying their weak biological explanations of God's amazing design, and I asked them to explain the eye, and prions. They were silenced at my illocution. Nonetheless, there were some who crept away with them. At their leave-taking, we cautioned them about the machine people, but their flesh was weak, and the food the machine people had brought was a temptation they could not withstand, our simple oatmeal a sudden contrast.

We were only twelve of the faithful, a number whose significance occurred to us when we were nearly out of food. We had rejected the gifts of the machine people, knowing them for the enticements of the flesh that they were, and had held to our purpose. I had learned enough about God's will that I was testing viruses on myself, and my willing community, but although we might thrash around in agony, we had yet to find the right sequence. God stayed my hand at the right times and made sure I was ready and worthy to be His will on the earth. When I found what I had been seeking for nearly thirty years, I knew it instantly, without having to test it further. From its small vial, it burned with an intensity that would destroy evil in the world, and my hands trembled to see it.

I met with my faithful eleven and told them what God wanted, and handed them each a vial. We went to the gates of the sinful city and asked admittance; let them praise us for our betrayal of faith, and then— our plan informed by God's will and Jesus' love—we went to the twelve corners of the earth. Once in position, we each drank from our vial and mixed with the people.

Because they had turned their back on God and pursued the league of Satan down the pathways of sin, the machine people never knew apocalypse when it was in front of them. As more of them became sick and then drifted on their burning way to hell, the huge gap in their understanding became apparent. They sought in the material world for an answer to a spiritual problem, until their machine world collapsed.

I came back to my community, once I realised that I was going to live longer than my brethren. God's will is not done with me, and I am not yet able to ascend to Him and enjoy eternity with my brothers and sisters. I try to have sympathy for the minions of hell, but even though His grace can include such sinners, I cannot. I am eager to join my community in heaven, and to experience the glowing beacon of Jesus and the blinding light of God.

Although I am ready, God is not. I realized today that there is one more test for me. I had thought the machine people gone entirely, except for those colonists who went to hide on Mars before God's righteous judgement came upon them. I realised today that some of the machine people live on. I thought, in my mortal way, that the virus would have brought all of them low, but God has held a few back so that they might find His way. They have been seeking me. No doubt they miss the holy word of God, and only now realise their loss.

I will go amongst them tomorrow, and try to bring them to the Lord. How infinite God's wisdom that He would keep me, a humble and sinful servant, alive long enough to offer solace to the crying few who were left after the first rider came through. What comfort I have to offer is only the word of God. For there are three more riders to come, and I am only privileged to ride with one of them.

A Hospital in Latin America
Julia Hones

IT was close to midnight. I had just sat down to finish my progress notes when there was a gentle knock on the door.

'Excuse me, Dr Parella. Ana would like to talk to you,' Gladys whispered, leaning through the open door.

'I saw her less than half an hour ago.' Tired, I wanted to finish my notes.

'I know, but she's really worried and insisted that she talk to you.'

'Okay, I'll be there soon.' I put down my pen.

The white hospital light seemed dim as I walked along the gloomy corridor to Ana's room. The weight of exhaustion pressed on my shoulders and back; my eyelids felt heavy. I knew it was a transitory state, the calm that preceded the storm of adrenaline that would make me feel invincible, ready to face anything.

Ana shared her room with three other patients. Turning on the light would wake the others, but I had no choice. I didn't want to have a conversation in the dark and risk stumbling upon something.

Ana was sitting on her bed, holding a picture, her back against the pillows. She smiled at me.

'Dr Parella, when can I go home? I meant to ask you earlier, but you were in such a hurry,' she said softly.

'You were admitted today because of your asthma. We need to see how you respond to treatment. I can't give you an answer right now.'

'I miss my child. I hate to be away from her,' Ana said, her eyes on the picture. I would find it difficult to forget the expression on her moonlike face.

'How old is your child?'

'Sofia is two years old,' she said, showing me the picture.

'She's beautiful.' I paused before continuing, 'I'm sorry I can't be specific with dates, but we need to take it day by day. We need to make sure that you're stable before we discharge you.'

I was getting anxious to leave the room. I wasn't a mother myself, and I did not know how to console her. Plus, I was craving for a few minutes rest before my shift turned busy.

The old lady next to Ana's bed—admitted three days earlier due to confusion—began to make gibberish sounds. I didn't want her to become agitated by our conversation so I rushed to turn off the light. I was about to leave the room when I heard a muffled sob. I turned on my feet and switched the light back on.

Ana's hands covered her face, but it was clear she was weeping. Sofia's picture had dropped onto her lap. I stood by her side, staring hopelessly.

'I didn't mean to be a nuisance to you, Dr Parella. I know you're busy,' she said between sobs.

I could not think of any words to appease her. All of a sudden, I felt silly and unable to deal with her emotions. 'You need to rest now,' I said, placing a hand on her shoulder. 'What a beautiful name, Sofia. Her eyes resemble yours,' I added, handing her some tissue paper.

'Thank you, Dr Parella. I appreciate your help,' Ana said. She settled down under the bed covers holding the picture of her daughter. 'I will try to rest now.'

I rushed to the nursing station where Gladys was scribbling some notes. 'Is everything okay? Let me know if you need anything.' I was hinting that she was in charge.

'Thanks, Dr Parella. I'll let you know,' she said firmly, without smiling. Gladys seldom smiled, and when she did it was usually sarcastic and meant to show the medical residents that *she* was the one in control. Her hostile and distant behaviour reminded everyone that she always won her battles.

I returned to my office to finish my progress notes. The air felt dry so I opened the window to let in a fresh breeze. The window looked over a patch of garden that was ringed by trees, their branches bathed in moonlight. In the distance, the city lights glowed. It was Friday night. I thought about all the other people my age out enjoying themselves. For a moment I felt wistful, but then rejoiced in the fact that my work was meaningful. I enjoyed helping others.

I'd finished my notes by the time Paul, my intern, came in. He walked slowly, his feet heavy, his eyelids drooping. I offered him help with his notes but he declined. Instead, I plugged in the coffee maker; I expected it would be a busy night.

We heard a knock, and the door opened slowly. Despite the darkness of the corridor we could make out Gladys's figure—her curly blond hair ballooned around her face.

'What's up Gladys?'

'Dr Parella, Ana's not well. Could you please come?'

'Sure. Is she crying again?'

'She's very short of breath. I gave her a couple of nebs but they didn't work. She's on the third one now.'

I slipped out of the office and hurried to her bedside. Paul trudged behind me, as he always did. We were an unsynchronised team. He did everything slowly, methodically, whereas I always rushed. When we walked along the corridor together, he would lag behind me. His hair, parted midline, was always neat and tidy whereas mine was often mussed, floating out of control over my head as I walked. The advantage of being on call with Paul was that Gladys would become more efficient in his presence. She was very fond of him.

Ana sat on the edge of her bed, struggling to breath. The mask was attached to her face. She seemed very sleepy. On listening to her lungs, I noticed little air entry and some wheezing.

'Ana, we need to transfer you to the ICU. You've been there before when you needed to breathe with the machine, the tube,' I said.

Ana nodded slightly. Her eyes remained shut.

'Paul, could you please draw some arterial blood?'

Within seconds, Gladys brought the kit and gave it to Paul, who bent down to take the sample. Gladys then turned to me. 'Dr Parella, we cannot transfer Ana to the ICU before talking to Dr Fitzpatrick. He is the one who has to decide if we can transfer her, not you.'

Without answering, I rushed to the nursing station and grabbed the phone. Gladys hurried behind me, warning that Dr Fitzpatrick did not welcome patients when he was on call. He would do anything to reject Ana. 'He doesn't like to be bothered with patients. He'd rather have them die on the medical ward,' she said. Her lips curled with contempt and vengeful triumph.

'That's his problem, not mine. I will do my job,' I told her.

'Hello, this is Dr Parella, the medical resident. I have a twenty-five year old patient here with an asthma exacerbation. She's not responding to medical treatment and will need to be intubated.'

'Really?' Dr Fitzpatrick's voice was sarcastic. 'You should come here and tell me all about the patient before I make a decision.'

'I'd rather not waste time.'

'You will have to, Dr Parella. I don't need to remind you that *I* am the one who makes these decisions.' He hung up the phone.

'Are you going to call the head of the department?' Gladys asked.

Just as in the army, hospital hierarchies were not something to be ignored. We had to respect the chain of command. I called the chief of residents. No response. My next move was to notify the head of the department. To my surprise, he answered my call.

'Do whatever Dr Fitzpatrick tells you to. I can't do anything about this,' he said.

Before meeting Dr Fitzpatrick, I approached Ana again. She was very sleepy and appeared detached from her surroundings. Paul stayed with her while I set off to the intensive care unit to meet Dr Fitzpatrick.

I walked briskly along the corridors and landed in his office without knocking. He was flipping through the pages of a magazine. As soon as I stepped in, he looked up with a grin.

'So what do you have for me, Dr Parella?'

I summarized the case swiftly, concluding that Ana Martinez needed to be admitted to the intensive care unit to be intubated.

'I will have to teach you, Dr Parella, how to take care of your patients,' he said, shaking his head and staring at me. I took a deep breath.

'What do you mean, Dr Fitzpatrick? We did everything we could, as I just explained to you in detail.'

'You don't know how to do a nebulisation. I will have to go to the ward and show you how to do it, *little woman*,' he said, the grin never leaving his face. His attitude set my mind on fire, but I kept my composure.

'I've got an arterial blood sample,' I said. I suspected that would be enough evidence to support the decision to transfer her.

'Fair enough, let's go to process it.'

We reached the device quietly amidst the orchestra of alarms in the intensive care unit. I plunged the syringe into the machine while he continued to lecture me with a litany of recommendations on how we had to do our work properly.

Within minutes I had the results and quickly scanned them before reading them to Dr Fitzpatrick. The pressure of carbon dioxide in her blood was extremely high. It warranted endotracheal intubation straightaway. I proceeded to announce the results and, out of the corner of my eye, caught a glimpse of his fading grin.

Dr Fitzpatrick crinkled his forehead and gaped at me with bewilderment. 'Bring her to the intensive care unit, right now,' he said in a low voice.

A fleeting twinge of pride uplifted me, but the only words that slipped out of my mouth were a polite 'thank you'. Along the dimly lit corridors, my legs moved faster than my thoughts.

Being on call is like sailing the sea in a rowing boat. We have to cope with all kinds of unpredictable events—*tides*—that make the boat sway. We risk tipping over when we least expect it. On the other hand, there are times when the sea is so calm that we sail at ease and enjoy the interaction with patients, knowing that the peace of the ocean is something we can cherish but never totally rely on. We become doubtful and worried that some clues from a patient have been missed, and a storm may break out unexpectedly.

I checked Ana again, before the transfer. She was even drowsier.

The portrait of her daughter was lying on the edge of the bed, on the verge of falling. I picked it up and placed it on her night-table.

The girl's smile stuck in my mind.

Ana was admitted to the intensive care unit and intubated by Dr Fitzpatrick. We had accomplished our mission.

Three days later, I was on call with Paul. After another sleepless night, we sat to have coffee and write our progress notes. The twilight of dawn was just beginning to rise over the city.

'Did you know that Ana died in the intensive care unit?' he asked.

'She died?'

'It happened yesterday when the electricity went off. The back-up system didn't work,' he said. 'I was in the ICU and a nurse told me. I don't know more than that.' He proceeded to finish his notes with a solemn expression. His other hand held a cigarette; smoke spread and clouded the air. I sipped my coffee in silence, wondering about the absurdity of a twenty-five year old woman dying because the system had run out of power, and the image of a boat sprang back to my mind, the waves and the sea, and the lack of control we have over the ocean.

True Love

Diane Lefer

I F you are a cynic, as I am, criticized for looking at fellow humans with contempt—arguing, instead of all this mandated compassion, how about some *rigor* for a change?—you will understand these stories must be true as goodness is beyond my power to imagine.

Love Story #1

The night I slept with Ellis wasn't sexual—that would have been child abuse. His mother had thrown him out or was otherwise unavailable. He was *persona non grata* in the neighbourhood, suspect in burglaries up and down the block. He was using drugs. I didn't trust him. I said he could sleep on my couch. After all, there was nothing in my apartment worth stealing.

We ended up in my bed that night, fully clothed, when we were each too overwhelmed by our respective insomniac terrors to be alone. His teeth were chattering and so were mine. We got under the comforter but it wasn't enough. I got another blanket, then the electric blanket. We shook and trembled with pain that was too subjective and individual to so much as tickle the scalp of anyone else. In the morning we still trembled, holding tight and then something else happened. His heart began to beat more evenly and his breath, which had been coming out all night in syncopated whimpers or stopping altogether and then bursting out with an eerie *hoo-hoo* sound, was suddenly tidal and soothing and steady and the sound and rhythm of it calmed and regulated my own. His breath was the most beautiful sound in the world and nothing mattered to me more than that it stay that way.

Love Story #2

Eddie felt fine, no symptoms, when he collapsed at dinner. In the ER, they told him the cancer was already far advanced and inoperable. A month later he was dead, and at 3 am I boarded a Greyhound bus, heading south for the funeral.

Though most of the seats were empty, and though he said nothing, a stranger took the place beside me. I thought he'd want to talk, which I did not feel like doing. Instead, he took out a book (*Manchild in the Promised Land*), put on a pair of glasses, and started to read. He looked to be in his forties, around my own age. I wondered if he'd read it before and why he was reading it now. I remembered the impact it had on me back in the '60s. Suddenly I wanted to take it out of his hands and read it again.

He put the book away and tried to sleep. When his leg fell against mine, I didn't draw back. And then, as though prearranged, we slept together. Our hands never touched each other's bodies, but our heads fell together, my head on his shoulder or his chest, and with the movement of the bus, from time to time we reversed so that he lay his head on me, our breath joining, our legs comfortably pressed thigh to thigh. There was no erotic charge. At least I felt none and I believe neither did he. I felt safe and grateful, protected in the way we like to think children are protected, and I wondered where he was going, what pain or need was in his heart that we both felt the need to offer and receive comfort. I was sure our need was the same, and that's what made the pressure of body against body, his warm breath on my face, mine on his throat, a stranger's head on my breast, the most unpresumptuous and welcome of gifts.

Love Story #3

Philip had a twelve-year affair with a married man he'd met in the park. They met regularly once a week for sex without either ever knowing the other's name.

'Just because you don't know his name doesn't mean you don't have a relationship,' I said.

He said, 'Men don't need to be emotionally attached to enjoy sex.'

'Neither do women,' I said. 'But when you have sex with the same partner for more than a decade, if there's no emotion attached, it gets boring, doesn't it? Don't variety and novelty win out over familiarity? Don't you need to care about the person for him to keep turning you on after so long?' I found myself arguing with him because what I really wanted to know was: What about his wife? Do you practice safe sex? Is any sex safe enough? Instead I said, 'I think you have a relationship with this guy whether you know it or not.'

Philip said, 'He held me when my father died. I was upset and he knew something was wrong. I started crying, and he didn't know why, but he held me.'

'See,' I said, glaring at him, wishing the triumph of being right would overcome the wash of jealousy.

It's not that I've never loved. I had a suicide pact with Lee. If one of us did it, the other would follow. That's what kept me alive, that I wanted him to live.

YOUR FAMOUS PINK RAINCOAT
Susan F Giles

WHEN you walk into the carriage a moment passes where I almost smile. There is a sense of occasion that surrounds a coincidence this unfortunate that it twists in my heart and feels like luck. Then I catch your eye, just for a second, and I remember. I turn to the window, pretend to watch the fields bleeding past, and focus on the pink blur of your reflection as you take a seat across the aisle.

I am surprised that your pink coat still fits, that it's still in one piece. It was old when we met ten years ago, and it wasn't expensive; it was impressive it lasted as long as we did. That it outlasted us, proved more robust than our happiness, is kind of insulting.

Definitely upsetting.

We are standing at the bar. I notice you immediately. Even in the hot, dense crowd it is hard to miss your hair, the thick auburn cloud swept away from your face with an emerald band. I want to smile, to move closer, but there is no space. The bodies surrounding us are crushing: behind, beside, against. There is a surge, a heavy man forcing his way through, and the edge of the bar digs into my chest, under my ribs, and I can feel my breath catching, escaping. Flecks of black, silver, dance in my vision and I am falling.

You are a stranger when you catch me. You scream at the barman for water, for help. I may be a short, light woman, but so are you, and you can't get me through the crowd. Someone takes pity on us, someone bigger and stronger, and pulls me backwards, to where the air is slightly cooler and the pressure slightly weaker. And then the hand disappears; this someone assumes you are my responsibility and ducks out before I can become theirs.

Being able to breathe is almost a cure, but I start to weave my way to the door just in case. I don't realise you're following me until I'm outside; the slap of frozen night air sends me reeling again and, as I slip to the ground, your hand appears on my shoulder.

You ask if I'm okay. Offer to fetch me water, fuss until I grab your hand and drag you down to the step beside me. You call me bossy then fall silent when I don't reply. I stare at my feet, counting my breaths in slow, controlled batches of ten until the last of the stars fade from my vision. I start to shiver as the cold air takes effect, and a curtain of hot pink material sweeps my shoulders.

I am fascinated by the tendrils of hair that have escaped your hair band. Thin, damp strands cling to your face.

'God,' you say. 'What a state. I'm sweating like a horse.'

I nod without meaning it, thinking about the strands of hair, about tucking them behind your ear or back into the band, about brushing your cheek accidently and smiling.

'Thanks,' you snort. 'You're supposed to disagree, tell me I look lovely.'

My cheeks flush and I can't meet your eyes as I stammer, 'You *are* lovely.' The heat in my cheeks triples. I wait for you to laugh, dismiss me with a gentle pat on the hand and disappear back into the club. I wonder if I am still out of it when you lunge forwards, brush your lips against mine. When you pull back you are smiling, so sure of yourself.

As an afterthought you hold out a hand, 'I'm Martha.'

We are lying in bed. The sun is streaming through the balcony doors and we are stretched in the sunspots, lounging our day away just because we can. I am wearing an old Stones shirt, with a hole in the armpit and a rapidly unravelling hem. You are wearing the pink gingham underwear I bought you for Christmas.

'How,' you ask, not actually looking at me, 'do you manage to look cuter than me in a scraggy old t-shirt?'

'It's a gift,' I smile. I wait a beat before rolling over, but you are still poking your tongue out at me, all childish petulance that should not be as attractive as it is. I lean towards you. Downstairs the doorbell rings.

'Ignore it,' I plead, hooking a finger under the strap of your bra, but you are up and running to the door.

'It's the postman,' you call back over your shoulder. 'He might have something exciting.'

I hear the soft slap of your feet taking the stairs two at a time, then stopping halfway down. A curse and then the footsteps again, this time getting closer. Your arm sneaks round the door, gropes for a handful of material and finds the pink coat. You disappear again.

I hear the faintest of voices as you open the door, barely audible polite greetings, then a squeal, the door closing, and your feet on the stairs, quick and heavy. You barrel through the door and throw yourself towards the bed, landing in a heap of pink cotton and peach flesh. You wave a ripped envelope under my nose; the institution stamp is the only thing visible, but it is enough.

'I got it!' Your voice cracks and you bounce on the bed like a child on Christmas morning. I smile but it is thin. Though your joy is infectious, I haven't forgotten what this means, what a new job in a new city will mean for you, for us.

You clamber onto the bed, right up over me, and the excitement is still there but dimmed. You push your face against mine, so close I am almost cross-eyed looking at you, and your breath, stale with sleep, tickles my cheek.

'Looks like we're moving?' A question, not a statement. This is one of those big, life-changing moments I spend my time trying to avoid. Yet it barely takes a second for me to respond. With your excitement and my fear, it hardly seems a decision.

'Looks like we're moving.'

We are on the phone. You are outside work. I don't need to see you to picture you hunching your shoulders, ducking your head, and doing your best to burrow into your coat against the wind I can hear ripping through the trees.

I am in the kitchen, fingers knotted through the red telephone cord, staring out across our patch of grass. There is a bird on the lawn, small and sleek and black, digging its beak—orange like fire on this grey day—into the earth.

It is mid-morning and I have just finished my daily trawl of job-sites and local papers. I want to tell you about the jobs I've found, only admin and temping but a couple are based just opposite your work, and in my mind I'm already employed there. We cycle in together, steal quick smoking breaks in the street and meet for long lunches in the café three doors down. Golden toasted sandwiches oozing cheese, and thick crusty baguettes spilling bacon—guilty student indulgences to off-set this adult life we were so quickly trapped in.

'I'm sorry,' you say again. I nod and smile as if you can see me. 'I just can't afford to miss this meeting. Everyone's going to be there and if I get a chance to pitch...'

We both know what's coming, another moment in your career, another chance to step up. This is why we came here, to allow you these moments.

'Yes, I know, it's fine,' I tell you, almost convincing myself.

In my head I rummage through the cupboards for a lunch more exciting than cereal.

The wind gives another howl and through the kitchen window I see the willow branches snapping back. The blackbird on the lawn stands straight, tries to fight against the rush but loses. It flies away, nothing more than a few blades of grass caught in its beak.

'That weather sounds awful,' I turn away from the window. 'You must be freezing outside.'

'Just a bit! Count yourself lucky you don't need to leave the house anymore.'

I don't point out our skeletal cupboards or empty fridge. Dinner is my responsibility, the least I can do when I'm home all day. I will still have to leave, have to battle the wind with hands full of plastic, hair in my face. But, though my skin is already prickling against the thought of the cold, I don't remind you, don't shatter your belief that you're doing me a favour by cancelling our lunch. Instead I hum in agreement, searching for a pen to start my list.

'Look, I've got to go. It's cold, and starting to rain. I'll see you tonight, okay? I'll get away early.'

I hum again. You won't get away early, you never do, but perhaps you'll be on time and that's a start.

I am in bed, propped up by pillows. There is a book in my hand, a world of luckless romantics and women who should know better. It has been a while since I read a word and even the character's names float just out of reach, too distant for me to care. I am watching the ugly glass mantel clock you inherited from your grandmother. My eyes follow the slow, steady swing of its gunmetal pendulum while I think of everything and nothing.

Your key in the door shatters the midnight hush. I try not to tense or sit too straight, try not to look like I've been waiting for you. I strain to hear your footsteps on the stairs, the familiar creak and click of the stripped floorboards. Downstairs, a tap runs, a glass rattles, and I am desperate to come find you, to question your lateness. But I don't. Finally, I hear you on the stairs and force my gaze back to the book; read the same sentence thirteen times, counting every repetition of the word *eternity* that my eyes pass over.

I expect you to be exhausted, apologetic. Another day where you couldn't get away, where an extra hour became two, then three, and you hadn't stopped long enough to even notice. I swallow my anger; I squash it down beneath concern and sympathy until I'm ready to accept you. I imagine you with chow mein in one hand, destroying your diet, and shadows under your eyes, looking ten years older than when I saw you this morning.

You appear in the doorway, eyes sparkling, steps uneven and I realise I am wrong.

You take off your coat—hot pink nails to match the pink folds—and throw it towards the chair, the right direction but without any force so it falls in heap, a foot short. You have only a glass of water in your hand, and there is a smudge of red on your blouse where a drop of wine has run and, in that moment, I hate you.

'Oops,' you say as you notice me, still awake, still watching. 'Shit.'

We are at a picnic. Your company's idea of a bonding afternoon. I am not the only other half there. We are dotted in between you like chaperones on a school trip. All of us laughing, smiling, nodding as if we are entertained by elaborate anecdotes about clients we have never indulged and bosses we have never ignored.

Every so often you turn and ask if I am okay, your voice, a rush of warm air against my cheek. I nod in reply, lying because I should be having fun, because I chose to be here. But my smiles are shaky and even you—happy, safe in the comfort of your friends—eventually notice something is wrong.

'You look cold,' you say, handing me your coat. I slip it on because it is easier than explaining the truth behind my discomfort. You look like you're about to ask more, push until my resolve cracks, but then another story starts; a man with over-gelled hair and cultivated stubble telling of a liquid lunch that became a liquid dinner. It's all so irrelevant that I can't stop myself from tuning out. My fingers pull and tease at a loose button on your coat, picking greedily at the thread until it unravels completely and the plastic falls into my hand. A flush of guilt, of regret, and my gaze darts to your face. I am expecting recrimination. An apology waits on my lips, but it goes unsaid just as the missing button goes unnoticed.

Against my hip a phone buzzes. A number that isn't familiar but can only be one person.

I whisper in your ear, 'Got to take this.' You release me with a nod, still focused on the flailing hands of the storyteller.

The news is not good. The usual platitudes, excuses. *There were so many good applicants, we were really spoilt. On any other day.*

I tell I them I understand, hoping they don't hear the cracks in my voice, the catch in my breath. There will be other paperwork to file, other phones to answer; I don't want to let this rejection bother me.

I hang up, turn back to the group I can hear cackling across the field. Your head is thrown back, your neat, tight plait swings with the laughter that I wish was fake. Fake because I can't remember the last time you laughed like that.

I wrap my arms around myself, fighting not to resent your laughter, your success. The coat feels heavy, your bunch of keys weighing it down.

This time the decision stretches out, and I feel every inch of unbearable significance in my action. The words of The Clash echo in my head and, for the first time that afternoon, I feel the pull of a genuine smile. I go.

We are arguing in the kitchen. It starts with something small—a moment's anger over a missed phone message—that swells and spreads until every grievance we've ever felt is storming out. Suddenly, I am screaming words I'm not yet ready to share.

You are stunned, stand perfectly still and stare at me. You are still in your shoes and coat. The space where the button used to be is a smudge of pink brighter than the rest.

'What?' you say, eventually. As if the words *I am going back home* were too quiet to hear. Even when I repeat them slowly, clearly, you just shake your head as if they don't make sense.

'To be a teaching assistant, but can't you do that here?' Your voice is too high, too sharp, and it scratches. Your expression is true disdain at my choice, at my future, and that's enough to drown out my guilt.

Of course I couldn't get the same job here. It might not be a lofty career path, demanding sacrifices and never ending days, but it is still one I am not qualified for. It's a job I've been offered purely for who I know, an irony I imagine you'd enjoy if you could see it. But all you can see is my desertion, your loneliness.

'No, I really can't. And I can't stay here. Not anymore.'

Silence aches between us. There should have been fireworks, begging and promises. One last attempt to rescue our life and turn three years into four, into five. Instead there is the ticking of an egg timer, the flick and hiss of the pasta water boiling and us, waiting.

When you finally speak, your voice splinters round the words. 'You're leaving.'

This time it is a statement not a question.

When you stand to get off the train, there is a moment where I almost stop you. Almost catch your arm, ask the questions running through my mind: questions of your life now, of the tattered leather suitcase by your feet, and why your hair now sweeps against your jaw, smart and neat and tamed.

When you step onto the platform, your tattered pink coat is bright against the grey station walls. You pause for a moment. Check for belongings or your ticket. Check where you need to go now.

Don't Break my Heart
Charlotte Comley

PALE white belly fat hangs over black lace thongs. Orange peel thighs abound, and large saggy breasts balance on rotund tums. Men with spots on their backs and grey chest hair walk around the room. How can anyone find this exciting? My husband's palm is sweating and he gives me the toothy grin that I'd once, at nineteen, found attractive, but at forty-nine, I'm beginning to hate. His hand leaves mine as he greets Fiona Davis. The woman handles food for a living, and I sometimes fantasise about reporting her to the grocery store where she works. I'm sure they wouldn't want her on the bacon counter if they knew how she spent her weekends. Even naked she smells slightly of ham.

I ignore Reggie's smile. Every week he tries to slide his way over to me. And even though I know my husband is just as keen as he is, I hold Reggie directly responsible, him and his stupid lock-ins and stories, putting ideas into my husband's stupid head. Thirty years of marriage, two children and one little grave. We were still together. Some say we had married too young, but until eight months ago I was happy. I was worried about the credit card bills and the kids, but happy.

I watch dispassionately as my husband pushes his tongue down Fiona's throat. She is older than me, fatter than me, smells of bacon, yet he is here with her, his fingers searching a mass of pubic hair.

Crystal bowls on the coffee table contain condoms, my suggestion, and tablets, some blue (not my suggestion). Each week someone gets to choose the music and the way Reggie is swaying at me, I presume Barry White is his choice.

A hand grabs my forearm and for a moment I panic, then I realise it is Rob. I let him guide me to the conservatory. It is cold. The lights are turned off, and a curtain drawn between the glass room and the living room. Reggie and Dorothy aren't that keen on people coming into this room. We often wonder if it's the neighbours watching or the heating costs they worry about. Rob pulls the cushions off the sofa and throws them onto the tile floor. We sit down and pull the quilt over us. With the lights off, we can see into the garden, the patio furniture is neatly covered. The house looks very presentable to the outside world.

Thankfully, Barry White's deep voice obscures some of the grunting from next door.

'I saw your photographs displayed in the library, they looked great.'

'I sold two,' Rob said.

'Oh, well done. You see, I told you.'

'I know I'm no Bailey, but it was great to know someone wanted my work. Not that I would ever be able to give up the day job. Did you see the article in the paper?'

'I did. I'm so proud of you,' I say, pulling the quilt up.

The curtain opens slightly, and we hold our breath, whoever it is sees an empty room and goes away. We smile at each other; these moments of feeling ridiculous and awkward are always near the surface. A veterinary nurse and an accountant, both old enough to know better, shivering naked on a tile floor, ridiculous.

'So what did the doctor say?' I ask.

He smiled 'You were right. It was just a cyst, but since she's been into this, I worry.'

I nod. *Damn right,* I want to say. I changed my washing powder, got a rash, and was convinced I'd caught some disease. Not that we ever made love any more. He usually wants me to tell him about my night—I always make something up—while he masturbates. Once this started intimacy disappeared. *It's just sex,* he says. *We married so young, never had a chance to experiment, this will make us closer.* I realise that he's going to do it with me or without me, nothing I say or do will change that.

At first it was just me with the awful Reggie, and him with Dorothy. And I, fool that I am, keep thinking that there will be an end to it.

I hear laughter from next door. Another Barry White track starts; I desperately try to remember the name of the song. As I listen to the lyrics, the title—*Just the Way You Are*—comes to me.

'Karen, are you alright?' Rob asks.

I realise I'm crying, tears roll down my face. I do this a lot these days. These parties make me question everything. I look back at everything in our marriage. What am I doing wrong? I think making love should be intimate, special. I know about the magazines under the bed, and the late night internet sessions. But I pretend I don't and put it down to something men do. It makes me question though. Am I not enough anymore? He says he stills finds me attractive, but how can he, if he wants to do this?

Sure, I'm not nineteen anymore; my body is softer, rounder after the children. But some of the women he has sex with are plain ugly. And now it isn't even enough to have sex with other people, he would like to add a new humiliation.

'He wants to watch me with another man,' I say.

Rob nods, he is sad.

'She does, too.'

I try not to let my face curl up in disgust but I can't.

'Hell, I can't do that; I couldn't even with a woman I didn't know, but hell—'

Comprehension suddenly dawns on me. 'You mean you and another—'

'Yes,' he says before I finish.

And then it hits me, like some sudden rush of understanding. It is quick and painful like chlorine up your nose when swimming.

This road will never end.

I will constantly be asked for one more thing. It is eroding away who I am. And then I realise something else and the tears start to flow again.

'You won't be here after tonight, will you?' I say.

He avoids my eyes and stays silent for a moment.

'How did you know?' His puzzlement is genuine.

'Because I know you,' I say, realising how well I *do* know Rob.

Every week we talk while our pretend friends and partners have sex in the next room. I know about his highs and lows, his dreams about photography, his worries. I can list what he reads and what he watches on television. His hair is getting long but he hates going to the barber, he will put it off until it tickles his ears. I know these things about him, things a *wife* would know.

I tell him things I used to tell my husband, like how I worry about our son working two jobs to pay for university, and how I cry when we put an animal down at work.

'Karen,' he pauses, this is difficult for him. 'I was wondering if you would like to have dinner with me.'

I married at nineteen. My husband and that bastard Reggie are the only men I've ever slept with. My throat is dry. I'm nervous and naked with him under a quilt. We should be outside with clothes on. I yearn for my underwear. Why do I feel as if I'm having an affair? We've never had sex, never kissed. My cheeks redden. Mixed feelings of anger, shame and flattery blend together and hurt like a physical pain.

Damn my husband to hell for doing this to me.

Rob's body is close to mine. He's started to play football again. Just five a side, but the exercise is making a difference to his body. I wish I agreed to go to Zumba with Sandie. I vow to start, and then catch myself. I shouldn't be thinking like this. He's only asking me to dinner.

'We could try that new restaurant in Oakland. I've heard it's nice,' he says.

I've heard it's out in the countryside and is a hotel. Rob toys with a spare piece of thread from the duvet. His shyness is endearing. I don't know what to say.

'You don't work Tuesday's, and I could take the day off,' he says, biting his lower lip. 'I've only stayed around this long for these chats. I've come to an important decision. I want to talk about—'

The curtain opens. My husband stands naked, his penis flaccid, and he smells of sex. He is carrying a stick with a pink feather on the end. Reggie is with him. The light streams into the conservatory. Our cold but safe sanctuary. Anyone looking out of their window would be able to see in.

'Mystery solved, it's not the neighbours watching that bothers him, he's just too tight to put the heating on,' Rob says.

I start to laugh. I laugh at the growing width of my husband's waist, his white body and at Reggie's pot belly.

Rob's hand finds mine. Our fingers interlock. *His* hand isn't sweaty.

My husband also laughs. I remember Mum saying he wasn't the brightest bulb in the box, and I laugh again.

'I thought I would join you,' he says, hopeful.

Reggie wets his lips with nervous anticipation. He wants to watch.

Rob helps me to my feet. We have the quilt around us but it doesn't cover us completely. I can feel his naked body, warm next to mine. He does not smell of sex, or body odour or *ham*. My husband nods at me, and I am sad, sad down to the marrow of my bones. He can leave me now. I will not mind. I will not argue or cry.

I turn to look at Rob; his eyes are brown, like my old Labrador. The comparison does not displease me. I loved that dog. He was faithful.

'I'm going to go now,' Rob says.

I nod.

And then Rob does something that surprises me. He puts his hand on my cheek. His head comes closer. I can see that he is nervous. My head goes toward him and we kiss. Our lips are warm and dry. I feel a soft tingle of love, respect, and something else. Something I didn't think possible in this house. Desire. I feel desire for this man.

'I think I would like dinner,' I say.

His smile is wide and honest.

Rob looks at my husband. 'Please can you take my wife home and let her know that I'll be staying in a hotel. I'll call to arrange a time to pick up my things.'

'No,' my husband says.

I let Rob put his arm around me. I smile up at him.

'No,' my husband says again, truth dawning.

The children are at university. They will be okay. I am surprised that this is my first thought.

'No,' my husband sounds desperate now. 'It doesn't work like this. It's just sex. It doesn't count. It doesn't have anything to do with your heart.'

Our Relationship with Thieves
Kati N Hendry

I came over once because we knew the twins were stealing from us and wanted proof. They'd stolen a deck of cards printed with Alice in Wonderland pictures and some pink seashells from Jen and Layla.

The others were scared to go under false pretences, even though you were their uncle and they knew you a lot better than I did. I was the oldest so I was the brave one. Besides, I thought the twins had something of mine—a gold ring my mom had bought me when I turned ten. It was pure gold, beautiful, huge for my chubby middle finger. And my sister was missing a heavy chain necklace, a present from her boyfriend. That made the twins' actions a felony, and made our response more than justified.

I geared up for the mission, which meant I took the unusual action of putting on shoes, and headed to your house. I knocked and waited for you to appear at the door.

'Hi, Martin! I was wondering—well, hoping—' I looked around the porch behind you, lost the nerve to look at your face. 'See, I was bored, and I don't have any cool toys to play with so I wanted to—'

My face was scorching, like a stove eye. This was strange; I didn't usually talk to adults. I wasn't precocious in the slightest. And I was humiliated by the lie that I played with toys. I never played with toys. Honestly, who does that? We ran around the woods and played pretend ninjas or spies or made salads out of grass and pecans and muscadines and tree bark. Besides, I would never play with anything those sissy little twins owned.

So, flushed with heat, I stammered, 'I wanted to know, would it be okay if I borrowed some of Tracy and Stacy's toys.' I finished in a stony deep sigh, defeated, head bowed.

You took a second to respond and were probably just as confused by this bizarre situation as I was, but also drunk I imagine, and maybe relieved that I wanted something easy to handle.

'Of course,' you slurred, red shiny lips, big smile, white teeth. A cordial host, you beckoned me into the house, arms wide, as if I stood yards away.

The house was empty but for you. That was strange too. I hadn't really been over since you divorced and lost the kids. The house seemed hollow and sad. I made a beeline for the back bedroom, knowing the twins had to stay where your kids, Jan and Jethro, used to. It was the only room besides the master bedroom. You used to run to it with your wife piggybacked, both of you screaming and giggling like mad, us kids screaming and giggling on the couch in the living room. Eventually, we'd all settle down with popcorn and Yoo-hoos for movie night.

On a mission, sharp and stealthy and fast as knives, I quickly found their room. You tried to guide me to the toy box, polite and helpful, but I was ahead of you. I was very rude, and I think maybe you hung back because of it. You took the hint, lost your confidence, felt the hollowness of the house again.

You must have known I wasn't really there to borrow toys. I was a weird kid and never talked. You knew that those of us left in the neighbourhood hated Tracy and Stacy. We were loyal to Jan and Jethro. A couple of weeks before, because they wouldn't stop following me, I'd led Tracy and Stacy about forty minutes into the eastern pine woods where the creek runs deep and barbed fences cut across squared lots. You need to know the right spots to shimmy underneath or the right tree to climb over. I didn't do a big complicated route or anything, followed the sand path once we were near the creek. I didn't hurt them, but then I ran, knowing they were big and slow and in flip flops. I knew they wouldn't be able to keep up. I could hear their jowly slobbery wailing behind me. Their big pink faces squished orb like over their pink shirts—cut off at the tummy to expose their navel. My sister wore hers that way too, only my sister was sixteen and beautiful and they were eight and awful.

The twins took over your life when they moved in. They broke Jan and Jethro's play set kitchen, then broke their swing set. Their mother sold our (technically Jan and Jethro's) trampoline because it was dangerous, and she shot us death glares anytime we came near when Jan was over for the weekend. Jan said their mom smacked her one day for bad-mouthing the twins—although I'm sure they deserved it! The worst part was that you let your new wife do it. After all that had happened, it was a betrayal.

God, we hated them.

I ploughed quickly and efficiently through their girly toy box. It was full of Barbie dolls and Caboodles. I realised my mission was not well planned. They probably had a secret hiding place. They wouldn't hide stolen property in the toy box. I knew after a few minutes that the search would be fruitless.

Suddenly, you appeared in the room with two plastic grocery bags. You held one open with both hands, still smiling, approaching giddily. As if this could be a peace offering you were proud to have come up with. I felt so sorry for you. I loved you and barely knew you and wanted to throw my arms around you.

I hated your stupidity for buying this ruse of a new family.

I tried to smile and accepted a shopping bag. I felt awful but kept up the act, planned to return the toys later, and hoped the twins would stay at their real dad's house for a few more days.

I tried to take just one or two toys, gingerly, something generic and not likely to be missed—a skip rope, a plastic hand mirror. But you were talking, slurring.

'How about this? This is nice. Take more, have more. *Please*. You like that?'

All the good stuff—the purple My Little Pony, the denim covered teddy bears you could write on with markers, the electronic Bop It.

I wanted to cry. I was trying to say 'no', to extricate myself. It was all too much. You were throwing yourself at the situation, the toys, me, the chance to give, to be of some use. Maybe you wanted a child in your house again, someone familiar from the time before the divorce and the drugs and the wreck, before the loneliness and guilt and pressing defeat.

Maybe I should have asked for fish sticks or a corn dog, or a push pop even—just ran into the kitchen and made myself at home, like most neighbourhood kids did at other houses. But even though I'd been there and ate your food and spent the night and slept next to Jan and Jethro and laughed on the sun deck while you drank Budweiser and horse played with the dogs, though I'd been there the whole time too, I was not talkative like the others. I didn't talk to adults. Whenever you came outside I'd clam up and stop playing. Suddenly I'd be studying a blade of grass or a tree branch while the others yelped and carried on.

I wanted to grab you and hug you, or laugh and say that all the toys were girly and stunk. Or even complain to you that the twins were little thieves, but you didn't need any more tension between you and your new wife. Jan and Tracy and Stacy caused enough.

I wanted to get my dad to come over and watch the game with you. But my dad didn't do things like that. I wanted to undo the rods they put in Jan's leg and the scars over your ex-wife's eyes from the crash. I wanted to make Jan trust you again. I wanted to sap away her mother's bitterness, get her out of the wheelchair, take away whatever was making her shaky; I didn't know about cocaine then.

You know I wanted to bring him back. We all did. It shouldn't ruin everything like that, so easily, so quickly. But it did.

Your eyes were deep ocean blue. They were so sad. I let you fill the shopping bag with the twins' best toys, but when you smiled so generously and started to fill another, I grabbed the bag and ran. I just ran out of your house and didn't even say 'bye.

When you died seven years later, no one was surprised. I was kind of relieved.

You were found by one of the workmen from your father's store. You hadn't shown up for a couple of days. It probably wasn't that unusual for you to skip work, but no one had heard from you so your dad sent someone to fetch you.

The coroner said you'd been gone at least two days. The funeral parlour hurried with the preparations. It was your liver, of course.

Tracy and Stacy and their mother were long gone. Good riddance, we'd said.

That marriage hadn't lasted a year. If you ever dated anyone after that, I didn't see them. By then all the other kids had moved away, and I was by myself. I stayed shut up in my room most of the time. I wouldn't know what your life was like during those last few years.

Honestly, it seemed like everyone was always just biding time. Life is supposed to go on, but this painful, slow-moving thing had to rip itself out of all of us first; it took a lot of guts with it when it fled me.

There was Jan to contend with when you died, and that was about it. It almost killed her all over again. I worried. She fought more with her stepfather for a few years. You left her a good inheritance, left her pretty much everything—there wasn't anyone else—so she was free to dangle over an open fire. I worried about the sort of people she was hanging around with. We ended up at different schools.

There wasn't much I could do.

At least that's what I told myself each time another eruption occurred, each time another kid or family from my childhood fell into the fire. They call it survivor's guilt but it always felt like I was the one left behind, left alone in the acres of woods and fields we once played in while everyone else moved on. I was left echoing old songs and games for years, when everyone else had grown up, gone on to juvie, to addiction, to pregnancy and kids of their own.

Way back then you were a really handsome guy to watch, a great and happy father. Bud cans and shiny red lips, white teeth, ocean mirthful eyes. I wonder if you knew that. You were a great father for a while.

We all thought so.

Lost to the Rising Tide
Kim Bannerman

N OVEMBER storms rearranged the shoals and left the beach changed, but with December came iron skies, flat waters, and a fog that softened the fir trees into grey felt features. A calm afternoon before the next front arrived.

Tracy and I wandered the shore, seeking treasures. We were nine and the best of friends. She was tall, lanky, with straight brown hair the colour of eel grass. She lived down the beach from me, and the coastline was our kingdom.

And what interesting gifts our winter sea gave us: bright blue buckets, swept overboard from passing trawlers; curious trash from Japan; swirling moon snail shells as big as a fist. We spent every afternoon this way and I thought that afternoon would be no different than the rest.

But I was wrong. I was studying a seagull bone, oblivious to the tears in her eyes.

'I got something to tell you,' she said quietly. Without waiting for my reply she blurted, 'We're moving across the country.'

'What?'

'We leave next month,' she choked, then ran ahead along the shore. She might've been crying, but I couldn't move. I felt punched. I stood there, deflated and numb and motionless.

My mind barely understood. *She was leaving.* Over and over, that lone and ugly thought repeated—until I heard her shriek.

'Ohmahgod, look!'

When my eyes followed her pointing finger, my heart forgot its grief. The fish on the shore was diamond-shaped, grey-brown and leathery. From point to point it was wider than we were tall. It lay on its back, showing the alien features of its pale belly and a thin straight tail like a riding crop.

I ran to her side and together we stared, mouths agape.

'What is it?'

'Idaknow,' she whispered with reverence.

It felt clammy to the touch. We tried to flip it and failed. It was too heavy for two skinny girls so we prowled around it, fascinated. The nose was an arrowhead, the edge of each thin wing was translucent and lacy, and the mouth lay far under its flattened head and gaped slightly in death. Small slits, tiny spines, and claspers nestled in the valley below its wicked whip of a tail.

Unspoken, we recognized the creature came from a world as cold and black as the moon. It told of dark, hidden depths where dolphins feared to dive. We volleyed ideas back and forth over the prone body. A sea monster? In our excitement, we forgot our sadness and didn't notice the tide coming in until it licked our gumboots. The water surrounded us.

'We're gonna lose it and we don't understand it yet!' Tracy grabbed its tail. 'Help me pull it higher!'

We struggled and heaved but it was rooted to the gravel. Finally, the water came and lifted it. Dead wings fluttered and the fish swayed, shuddered, and yearned to return to the sea.

'You can't go!' I screamed at it, at her.

Together we pulled, but the monster's weight threatened to drag us with it; so we relented to forces more powerful than us and let go, our hands slimy and salty. As the mercurial waters bore the beast away, we watched from the shore with tears streaking our faces, overwhelmed by our loss.

Ava, Leigh, Sarah, Minnie Annie, and Me

Zarina Zabrisky

THE air smells like Thanksgiving: roasting turkey, rosemary, and cranberry sauce.

The kitchen is hell. Hot, loud and sticky. The sink is overflowing with pans covered in grease and steaming water. The water sprays all over Max, our ginger cat. He's playing with a piece of lettuce on the windowsill. He jumps sideways and knocks over the pot of mint, and Ava shoos him with a mop, laughing. Stuffing crumbs and mustard are all over the floor, mixed with soil and mint leaves. Annie crawls unnoticed and finds a spoon under the stove. She thinks it's cookie dough, licks it but then bawls because it's baking soda.

This chaos happens every year as we get ready. Ava's the oldest. She's calm and cheerful despite it all. She always knows where everyone is. It's amazing how she can do everything. That's because she takes after Grandmother. I think she looks like her, with her frosting-blue apron and hair up in an old-fashioned bun.

'Annie, stop crying,' she says. 'You're a big girl now, a good girl. Here, get out of the corner. Don't suck your thumb! Put your doggie on the bed, like this, good girl. Woof's going to sleep now and Annie is going to take a nap, too.'

Annie is whining, but she lets Ava put her to bed and dozes off, thank God.

'Sarah, stop texting, sugar,' says Ava. 'Rolf will wait.'

Ava probably feels like she's the captain of a sinking boat.

'It's not Rolf, it's Gary,' says Sarah, twisting her mouth, her fingers clicking on the phone like crazy. Sarah is a bubble-head. She only thinks about guys. I wonder if she even knows it's Thanksgiving.

'Gary will wait, too,' says Ava, smiling. 'Minnie, it's not a good time for writing, my dear.'

'I'm writing a poem, leave me alone,' says Minnie. 'I'm sick of your kitchen nonsense. Where's Leigh? Make *her* help.'

Minnie's okay. She's always writing, her voice is quiet and she rarely speaks up. If we were all like Minnie, we'd have no problems. Leigh is the main problem, but no one seems to know where Leigh is.

'You know Leigh will never show up for this crowd,' says Sarah. I can tell by her voice that she's rolling her eyes while texting. 'She's probably outside smoking.'

Sarah's twenty-three, the closest in age to Leigh and mostly sides with her—although she never has a problem ratting her out.

Ava sighs and sets the table. She aligns the napkins, fine china, and family silver, singing as she works. She loves holidays and guests. Sarah is helping her, but still texting boys. How she can remember all those boys, I have no idea.

I watch from the couch. Boy, do I know that Ava needs help. We all need help. But I can't make myself move. I'm tired, inside and out, weary to my bones. I'm tired of all the noise, fighting, and fuss. I wish for once they would all just leave, disappear somewhere. So I can get some peace and quiet, read a book or sleep. I didn't invite the Lymans and Hobermans for Thanksgiving. I'm sure Minnie, Leigh and Annie didn't invite anyone. I never know the people Ava and Sarah invite. I have to mumble something if they start speaking to me. I'm sure they think I'm weird, but I don't really care. I don't eat turkey, and I hate pies, the whipped cream makes me sick to my stomach. If it were up to me, I'd cancel all holidays.

Sometimes I wish we had a guy or two here, maybe it would be different. Instead, I know exactly what will happen. Ava will make sure Annie is asleep in the bedroom. Then she'll line up everyone else, inspect hair, check make-up, all that stuff. Then they'll have an argument about what shoes to wear. They'll drag all the shoes out of the closet and just stare at them. Sarah will want red spiky heels, and Ava will ask her in a sweet, calm voice, 'Just for tonight, wear Mary Janes and cover your tattoo. Please sweetheart, for me.'

I've heard it all before. I can recite it by heart.

Maybe I should surprise them by finally jumping in and screaming, 'Get out of here, bitches, it's my place, get the fuck out of here with your damn shoes and the Hobermans.'

I can imagine Sarah hissing back. 'We live here too, you lazy useless bum!'

I can imagine Annie then waking up and screaming.

Leigh might even show up for the occasion, all loony and spacey. She's the nastiest, so who wants her?

Ava will go droning on about being a family. Listen to her, and you'll believe that we should work things out. Of course *she's* the one who goes to stupid therapy and smiles there for an hour every week.

Me? I just keep a low profile and sit on the couch, watching. They leave me alone, pretend I don't exist. Sometimes they really forget about me, I know it. I'm like a ghost in the closet, but I can see everything and hear everything. I understand much more than they know. I'm the spy in this asylum.

And then the Lymans and the Hobermans show up, all dressed up in plaid and grey jersey, their noses and bald spots gleaming. They unpack potato salad and a pecan pie with rum. Meanwhile, poor Max hides under the couch, playing with my slipper. Eventually he falls asleep.

Ava is happy. She gets to talk about the symphony and her jewellery class. She shows her rose garden to Mrs Lyman. Lily Hoberman eats all the salad she brought, as usual. Everybody's happy as fuck. When Max moves to the couch next to me, we both fall asleep and no one notices.

I wake up and the Lymans and Hobermans are gone. Ava must have stepped out with them, or maybe she's putting the leftovers in their car. Perhaps she's taking the trash out, or looking for Leigh. I have no idea. Minnie must be in the bedroom writing her poem, and Annie must be asleep because she's not crying.

So there's only Sarah at the dining room table. Who is going to do all the dishes and clean all the turkey bones and put away the leftovers? Max sits on the table chewing a piece of turkey, his head tilted to the side, sharp teeth tearing through the grey meat, juices dripping down on Ava's tablecloth. I see a china plate loaded with pecan pie and whipped cream. A glass of sherry with a red lipstick print sits next to it, and then I realize Sarah is not alone.

There's a guy—huge, fat, with crumbs of stuffing in his disgusting goatee. He must be Gary, or Rolf, or Will. She always has a new one and

I can never remember any of them. He's drinking sherry and yakking about football. I'm still sleepy. I'm about to say something but before I get my act together, Sarah is all over him. They are French kissing, and then the guy lifts her up and carries her to the kitchen. He puts her up on the counter and Sarah wraps her legs around his fat butt. I watch all this, and she pretends that she doesn't see me and doesn't even know that I exist.

But I *am* here, and I know she can see me through her half-closed eyes. She hopes I won't do anything. She pretends I don't exist, acts as if I'm nothing.

The guy starts humping her. She moans and I can feel how hot she is for him. I feel my own blood boiling and I hear a noise in my ears. The guy's puffing and I can feel his huge hot hands and fingers diving into Sarah's ass.

Is it Sarah moaning, or me?

Who is this guy? I've never seen him before. Is he a rapist, an intruder? Where is everyone when you need them?

'Get out of here,' I cry.

'Sarah, what's wrong, baby?'

I push him. He's huge but doesn't expect it. His clothes are messed up and there's cranberry sauce on his cheek. Or is it blood? Did I just cut him with the carving knife I'm holding?

'You're crazy,' he shouts. 'Crazy bitch!'

I scream, telling him to get out, my hand firm around the knife.

He pulls his pants up and runs out of the kitchen. Then Sarah is all over me, shrieking—can't she ever just speak? Why does she always have to scream?—'You fucking moron, I hate you, I hate you!'

And of course, Ava is back, her voice calm. 'What happened, what happened?'

Annie is up and crying and Minnie is here with her poem, and even Leigh is back and I can tell she's angry.

'I'll never get a boyfriend with all of you around,' Sarah yells. 'I'm sick and tired of this life! Every time I like someone you pull this shit! I'm going to kill myself this time, I'm telling you.'

I retreat back to the couch and stare through the window. It's dark outside. I'm getting hungry and just want some normal food, not this Thanksgiving crap.

'Calm down,' pleads Ava. 'Relax, let's all take a deep breath. Our therapist says the only way to survive is to integrate. He says we should focus on the body. Let's face it, we share this body.'

'I'm not sharing anything,' says Leigh. 'I'm my own person, you old fuck.'

I get up to go to the kitchen—I want a bagel with cream cheese—and Max catches my foot as if it's a mouse or a piece of lettuce. I step on his tail in the dim light and he jumps and howls. His teeth pierce into my ankle. It hurts like hell, and I shove him into the corner. I sit down, holding my leg, blood on my fingers.

All of a sudden the voices in my head are gone. It's just me, my blood, my fingers, and Max's silver eyes in the corner, like two tiny mirrors.

Maybe Ava's right. Maybe we should try to integrate after all.

THE COLOURS OF HER SOUL
Monika Pant

We found Mrinalini strange. Weird.

Her ways were odd to us and we were not, by any stretch of the imagination, conservative. In fact, we had come a long way, climbing the ladder so to speak, working and socialising in high places—in government service or in private business. We moved in circles that were the hallmark of modern, urbanised India.

We never commented on her belonging to a different social class, her lineage not in keeping with ours. We knew she couldn't help the circumstances she was born into. Nor did we concern ourselves with the different traditions she followed. *Those* we would have found quaint. Perhaps we might have even adopted a couple of her customs. After all, what else is marriage but an alliance between two ways of life?

The problem lay elsewhere. Mrinalini was a nonconformist, a wayward individual, a girl who kept to herself as if not part of the human chain of togetherness. Mrinalini was a grain against our social milieu.

To a tight-knit family such as ours—a family that ate together, went on outings together, shopped together, celebrated together—her behaviour amounted to rejection. Mrinalini seemed disdainful of everything we said or did.

She was always sweet to our faces, of course; she was not so naïve. Sometimes she would sit with us, but more often than not she remained isolated in her room and refused to engage in conversation. On such occasions we could hear her muttering and humming to herself. Other times she would take off on a whim to some godforsaken gathering of those who thought and talked as she did.

Yes, Mrinalini was odd, and we did not understand her.

Often she would sit on the garden swing, rocking herself to and fro—we'd all seen her. She would sit staring, hands trembling, a distant look shadowing her face whenever the call of a koel caught her attention. Once, in a rare talkative moment, she told us that the koel's plaintive cry haunted her, made her remember the night she came to us; a young bride to her husband's family. We weren't sure how to take such a comment, strange as Mrinalini was.

There was the time we were sitting on the porch, leafing through catalogues, trying to decide how to best coordinate our dresses for a family wedding, when Mrinalini's behaviour seemed especially unusual.

She picked up a butterfly from the grass; it was flapping its wings but did not fly away. Presumably it was hurt so she carefully placed it on a half-open flower bud.

A bit of blue stained her fingers, but when she tried to dust it off, like a memory, it refused to go. She started to walk inside, staring at her fingers as if in a trance. Suddenly, she looked up, startled that there were chairs laid out on the verandah. We were having tea and snacks. A little thrill ran through us, and we smiled at each other, assuming—or perhaps hoping—her baffled look contained some guilt, but she just continued to stare at us as though *we* were the ones who had lost our senses. Perhaps she suspected one of us of crushing the butterfly underfoot.

Nonetheless, we politely invited her to join us. She accepted the cup of tea and continued to stare at her fingers. One of us asked what she was looking at, but Mrinalini just shook her head, eyes downcast. She quickly drank her tea and left us.

Then there was the time we had relatives visiting from abroad. We were busy making the house presentable in spite of the dusty hot summer. Chandeliers needed wiping, floors polishing, divan covers replacing—but what put us off was the pained expression on Mrinalini's face while she helped. Even after our guests arrived, and all of us were trying to make them comfortable, Mrinalini remained aloof, standing off to the side holding the small bunch of carnations she'd arranged for the guest room.

Marrying into our family was an honour. We asked ourselves if she realised how lucky she was. One of the oldest families—the whole city knew of the Shankars. A modern family, we'd gone beyond the borders of superstition and age-old ideas. We made no restrictions on her. She could take up a job, wear what she wanted, adopt a Western lifestyle, go on holiday to upscale resorts, and give lavish parties—as we did.

And yet she continued to flout our ways, even when we tried to accommodate her. Like the time we delayed a prayer service because Mrinalini decided to go out without telling anyone. She must have heard us talking about her. When she finally arrived, she averted her eyes and kept her head bowed. But then the chant began and she acted as though the incense was making her head reel. We could see that she was hardly appreciative of what we did for her.

When she was diagnosed with cancer, we took turns to give her solace, to take care of her young children, to stay at the hospital overnight—even though we had to work the next morning.

If only she'd given some indication that she appreciated our efforts. But she never did, and we resolved to never inconvenience ourselves for such a person again. We thought that after her mastectomy she would show some humility and gratitude for life and family.

Mrinalini never wanted any show of concern over her health; we found it strange that simply asking how she was would upset her. She seemed to hate giving details of her discomfort, yet we didn't know how else to help. How could we assist her if she didn't let us know what she was feeling?

It was futile trying to help her; she would just run to the solitude of her room, retreat into her shell of pain. She callously rejected all our efforts to get her to enjoy herself and forget her misfortune.

Mrinalini never lost an opportunity to show that she was different. A trifle wild, a trifle sentimental, she wove in and out on the wings of impulse, living in the moment and revelling in it.

Very quickly she made our brother, her husband, speak the same language. Perhaps he was taken in by her charms or intimidated by her tantrums. She seemed to be biding time, like a panther waiting for the kill.

It was peculiar that she never agreed with our family traditions. Even celebratory events, such as anniversaries and birthdays, with family and friends were shunned by Mrinalini. She preferred dinner at an exclusive restaurant with just our brother and their children. We thought it weird that she preferred watching English films on television in the privacy of her room, to watching sitcoms in the family lounge. And how strange of her to go shopping alone! And why did she not show us what she bought? We always had such a great time displaying sarees and jewels in the drawing room, praising each other's choices. We wondered what she read, sitting alone on the garden swing while we held gossip sessions on the verandah.

In the early years, our uncle and aunt tried to help her adjust. They constantly asked her, 'Why have you kept your door closed? You should mix with all of us. How else can your new relatives get to know you—or you, us?'

But her reply was always the same, 'Uncle, I don't like anyone looking at my paintings before I have finished.' And then she would close the door and return to her *art*. Just like that, without even a courteous 'by your leave'. We found her behaviour very disrespectful.

Nor did she discuss any important decisions with us, such as whether she should take a job at a local school, or where she should enrol her daughter. Sometimes she just went off and left the children with her mother.

Mrinalini's children were also antisocial. They remained shy and withdrawn and in constant need of encouragement. She pampered her youngest daughter and wouldn't even allow her on the floor. We thought this ridiculous, how could a child learn to walk without crawling on the floor? But Mrinalini claimed it was unhygienic because everyone walked in with their shoes on.

We had voiced our concerns on a number of occasions, but things finally came to a head at a family gathering.

Mrinalini had dressed her youngest daughter in black; it was an inauspicious thing to do and, shocked, we told her so. We even suggested her daughter wear the pink dress she'd worn at a previous gathering.

Mrinalini looked towards her husband, probably hoping he would side with her, but he didn't. Instead, he turned away to talk to a guest.

We watched tears fill her eyes as she picked up her daughter and left the room. But something, some resolve, must have stirred within her because when she returned, her daughter still wore the black dress. After that, Mrinalini retreated further into her shell.

Standing outside her door we'd hear her painting. Harsh, swift strokes of the brush, the slap of paint on canvas. She painted in a frenzy, the only way she seemed able to express her thoughts.

We left her to it and appealed to her husband. But, little by little, our brother had become less ours and more hers. We tried to tell him; he indulged Mrinalini too much, but he just frowned and bowed his head.

Sometimes one of us would push open the door and ask if she wanted some tea or some dinner. She'd be sitting there, an unfinished painting abandoned, with the contents of her trunk spread out—books, cuttings, hand-made cards, letters tied with string, a half-done sketch of Raj.

She wouldn't look up, even when we spoke. She would just sit there with a faraway look on her face, caressing the items. It was as though we were intruders into her world. Watching her, we had the sense of shifting sands beneath our feet.

We were surprised when her paintings received recognition; she never shared her joy with us but continued to shut herself away, painting furiously as though running out of time.

We did not understand why newspapers gave glowing accounts of her work. Her paintings seemed incoherent and disjointed to us—disproportionate faces, eyes strangely angled or absent, grotesque even. And yet, a force emanated from the images that made us look away.

As time passed, Mrinalini became like a ghost inhabiting our mansion. Her wild energy, impulsive laughter, and even her strong reactions to our ways, slowly disappeared; it was as though all her thoughts and feelings poured in a steady stream into her art. Her paintings sapped the vibrant colours of her soul until, one day, she vanished from our lives. All that remained on her crumpled bed sheet was a long strand of grey hair and the lingering perfume of jasmine.

PONY HARRIS
Tanya Jacob Knox

WE met Pony Harris in line for *The Rocky Horror Picture Show* in West Los Angeles back in our early twenties. She was this short fat girl with no apologies and a square, flat face that looked remarkably like a bull. Piercings up her ears and one through her bottom lip. A voice that was dull and funny. She liked riding horses.

Her smile sat strange in our stomachs. She was intimidating. Fascinating and real, both untouchable and undesirable. Pony was gay early. She never did the bi thing. She liked women and she looked it. She had these big glasses with thick black frames that made her look very smart and slightly atrocious. But she never hooked up with anyone and not many of us knew her name.

And when we all went to Bondage Ball, no one invited Pony. And when we glammed up for dancing at The Standard, she was left behind. We thought she was alright but there was just something about her.

Those lazy days smoking cigarettes on faded couches, drunken nights in unlocked bedrooms. We invented casual sex, naked and beautiful and young. And surreal. Distracted by muddled waters of expectation. Were we wild or boring? Beautiful or awkward? All our sad parties and nervous laughter behind flat beers and forced smiles. And there was Pony, always alone.

Eventually she left Los Angeles and moved to Oregon where she bought a cheap house and fell in love with a woman who mirrored her looks and interests. We followed her life online; from her nervous and poetic scribbles to her weird hairdos, tattoos and piercings. We follow her still, recently watching her graduate as a funeral director.

Now we know what that strange feeling was. Her wit and style, her matching bright-eyed bull face; she tailored her appearance and mannerisms into a precise replication of who she was on the inside. She reminded us all we had such a thing. An inherent, atavistic reaction to see a person decorate their inner self, their soul, churned in the pit of our stomachs.

We don't feel sorry for Pony. Not for how we ignored her or for how she must have felt. We feel plenty sorry for ourselves though, and the years wasted on definitions of life and standards of beauty that we made into our own Frankenstein. We believed in the fantastical taut skinned reality created in drunken moments, incarnations of idealized youth: careless, dissociated, and superficial. We feel sorry for ourselves every time we see her—she was just one of the many treasure chests that sat directly under our floorboards, discovered too late.

ISLAND ROCKS
Dora L Harthen

SENTINELS, slick with rain and mist from the sea, we line the coast. Jagged, our dark shale is lethal. No beacon cuts through the blackness of night or the fog of day; there is no safe haven here, no help for the stricken. Alone, we watch and wait, bearing witness to the passage of time. After years of silence, our peace is disrupted. Incessant chatter ripples across the tide and echoes against our granite backs. A large craft anchors in the distance beyond our rocky stacks. Tentative steps taken from a bobbing dinghy announce the new arrivals.

Once there was a time when they were all so eager to leave. Hardships endured for centuries grew intolerable to the dwindling number of inhabitants. We remember the first. We remember the last—intrepid explorers, faithful monks, crofters and seafarers. All struggled to survive. We remember the final two. They refused to leave and waved off the last of the evacuees with a dismissive shrug. The old woman died two months later. Her husband held out for a full year.

A strange spectacle, these seasick tourists with their clicking cameras. They are not the hardy island folk who once graced our land. The captain brings them—he understands us, knows our ways—yet tries to protect us. He lectures the visitors about preserving our wildlife, our heritage. His insistence is often met with sniggers and rolled eyes and a degree of arrogance as they pose for pictures taken with phones and tablets. They say they have to tweet, to Facebook, to share the experience of their retreat. Soon they realise there is no signal for their digital toys. They can't connect with their world. Struck by the reality of isolation, they become subdued, nervous, twitchy. Some check their watches, eager to leave. Others laugh nervously when the captain says he'll return to collect them.

'When?' someone asks.

'Don't worry,' he replies. 'You have plenty of time to visit the ruins.' He pauses then, looking up at the sky. 'You might want to start with the monastery, mind. That way you'll be back by the church and schoolhouse before those clouds roll in. That's the best place to be when a storm hits. If that happens, wait there.' He climbs into the dinghy and turns to face the bewildered group. 'It'll probably blow over. Keep an eye out for the gannets. There's a big colony here. Impressive wingspan,' he spreads his hands. 'They nest up on the stacks. If you're lucky you might see one dive.' With a quick snap of the rope, he looses the dinghy from the makeshift jetty and shoves off.

Water laps over our sides and when his small boat comes close, he uses an oar to push against our backs. The group of visitors watch until he is almost halfway to the anchored vessel. Then one of the women pulls out a green guide and opens it to a post-it marked page. She reads to the group, telling them about the ancient village, the black houses, the peat banks, and the stone cleiten scattered around the island.

'Cleiten were used to store food and fuel,' she says, looking up. 'Let's head to the monastery ruins.'

Her companions smile politely but when she launches into a spiel about Viking marauders, a few hang back, saying they want to see the village first. A young woman, clearly bored, rolls her eyes and pulls her partner away. They head in the opposite direction, their whispers and laughter lost in the groan of the wind. Intrigued, expectant, we watch the group disperse. We listen as the woman with the guidebook doles out a potted history of our land. She moves on to our natural resources and wildlife. *Puffins...Fulmars...Gannets...*Once the islanders' source of food and fuel, now an ornithologist's dream. Her two followers nod encouragingly. One pulls binoculars from his rucksack. She mentions the submerged caves around our coastline, and we recall the divers that come every year. They pull themselves up onto our backs, slippery and wet. Their flippered feet tickle our sides. Our attention wanders from the woman with the guidebook to the small group wending their way through the village. Without a guide they explore at random.

We hear a yell, at a distance from the village, and our attention shifts. The couple, laughing only moments before, face each other. The young woman sits on a blanket. She clutches her knees and cries. Her partner stands a few feet away. His stance is angry, aggressive.

We watch as suddenly she jumps to her feet and runs away. The man starts to follow but she turns and screams, her words ricocheting off our granite. '*Leave …me…alone!*'

The man hangs back until she is almost out of sight, and then he trails after her. He keeps his distance, waiting until she calms down before approaching. We watch them closely; they are near the edge of a precipice where our rocky striations steeply give way to the sea. For a moment they stand and look down. Foam gathers around our stony shore as the tide crashes in. She lets him put an arm around her, but it's not long before they argue again. Their words mingle and catch in the wind. *A baby…impossible…my wife…I can't leave…How could you let this happen?…But you promised…You said you loved me…What am I to do?*

We watch as she shouts and pummels his chest. He grabs her wrist and they struggle. Angry, she lashes out, pushes, and he loses his balance. We know what could happen and try to hold firm, but he is heavy and falls too close to our edge; it gives way. Suddenly he is falling, arms stretched wide, flailing, and she is screaming. His body crushes against us as we break his fall. She tries to reach him but it is too steep and she cannot find a way down. In shock, she collapses to the ground and sobs.

We watch as minutes turn into hours. Finally, her tears cease. '*It's my fault. I'm sorry.*' Her voice is so faint we barely hear it. She collects herself and heads toward the village to find the others. We look on as they try to console her. Someone suggests trying to retrieve the man but we are an obstacle to navigate, and they don't have any equipment. What could they do even if they were to reach him?

They wait and we watch. Eventually the captain returns and the coastguard is called. The woman is questioned briefly. *It was an accident… we were walking…he just slipped…it happened so quickly.*

As we stand with the icy tide bashing our sides, words slide smoothly off our backs and truth lodges between our crevices. Stoic, silent, we can do nothing but bear witness. Watching and waiting through the passage of time.

OUR SOMETHING SAID
Zena Shapter

IN all our hearts lies the fear that someday our children might be taken from us. For some of us though, it's more of a knowledge. We live waiting for the day it will happen. We're not sure how exactly it will happen—after all, our children are only three, four, maybe five—yet they behave so differently from others that the idea of losing them feels inevitable.

It's why we hope no one sees us as we leave our community health centres. The more people who know that our children are in counselling, the more people will judge. Our parenting will be blamed, and people will say we're the ones with the real problem, projecting it onto our kids. In part, they may be right. But until we know that for sure, we don't want to be judged. Our children's demise is hard enough to bear as it is.

So, on the road outside the centre, we hurry our families into cars, checking over our shoulders as we always do. Is today the day we'll be spotted?

'Let's go!' we mutter to our husbands, who aren't quite as anxious.

'Home?'

'I don't know. Yes, I suppose. Let's just go.'

When our husbands pick the beach route home, buzzing down the car windows so the kids can watch the surf, we're mad at them for not understanding—until we realise it's okay if someone sees us now. It'll just look as if we came from the playground around the corner. So we allow ourselves a moment and breathe in the salty sea air, exhaling slowly.

In the silence, our husbands try to make us feel better. 'You know it's not us, right? Our parenting is fine.'

Not moving our eyes from the horizon, we nod. 'But we have to try.'

'By doing what?'

'I don't know.'

Our counsellors have told us to spend at least ten minutes a day playing 'special time' with our children They say the same thing to all of us, though we don't know that at first. We think their advice is specific to our individual situations. So we listen when we're told to ensure our children lead the play. We don't ask our children questions or pass judgment—including praise—we just make observations, like we've been told to do. *He has picked up a blue block, now he's putting it on top the red block.*

Sometimes, though, our children throw their Thomas trains across the room, just because they wouldn't line up in an exact straight line. Our children are starting school in a few months, yet if we give them the wrong colour plate, they push it onto the floor, food and all. Sometimes they have panic attacks if their socks aren't pulled absolutely flat against their skin. Often they just sit in the pushchair and tell us they're sad. Silently, we endure it. We know it's not our children's fault.

'He's depressed,' our counsellors tell us with a shrug. 'He probably always will be. It's just a matter of degree.'

Still, there must be something we can do? Something has to work. It shouldn't be this hard. Thinking back, we remember something the counsellors told us at our first appointment. Eldest children can be highly sensitive to family stress, so for the next few months we become adamant about minimising stress at home. We put our children into preschool on different days so we can spend quality time with each of them. Some of us even stop work for a while.

'Can we afford that?' our husbands ask when we tell them.

'Can we afford not to?' we reply.

Months later at bath time, our youngest child, Sarah/Selina/Santi might be playing with a yellow boat, or a pink foam letter 'M' in the water. Her brother, Daniel/Michael/George, will seem happy enough playing with bubbles or watching the water swirl. Yet, the second we turn to reach for the Top-to-Toe wash, there's a scream.

'Daniel, give the boat back to Sarah, please.'

'No.'

'You can play with it when she's finished. Right, Sarah?'

Sarah/Selina/Santi nods.

'See? Now give it back.'

He won't move.

'Daniel?'

No response. He's been like this all day.

'Right then,' we prise the toy off him and give it to Sarah.

'No!' Daniel yells.

'I did warn you, Daniel.'

He splashes water into his sister's face. She starts crying.

'Daniel, say you're sorry!'

'No. I want her to go away!'

'Go away? Where to?'

'The desert.'

'What, all by herself?' We chuckle then, thinking he couldn't possibly mean it. 'With no Mummy or Daddy?'

He nods.

'Don't you love her, Daniel?'

'No!'

Weeks later, we'll be called back to the centre. Our kids' preschool teachers have completed their questionnaires. They say our little ones are withdrawn there too. They don't join in the singing or dancing; they prefer to sit by themselves rather than participate in group activities. We've always thought of our children as independent, but now they're called vacant.

'Isn't that just him knowing his own mind?' we ask our counsellors, picturing his sister—Sarah/Selina/Santi—twirling to *The Wiggles* with the other kids at playgroup. 'Sarah's not like that, so how can it be our parenting? Are you sure it isn't anything more…medical?'

Our counsellors shake their heads, bashing dangly earrings against brown or blue polyester jackets. They've seen this a million times before. Parents in denial. 'Nothing medical causes behaviour like his. And you've been to the doctor?'

'Many.' We needed to be sure.

'You did move around a lot when he was young,' they remind us.

We nod then, because when Daniel/Michael/George was seven/eight/nine months old, our husbands changed jobs, or our landlords increased the rent, or our apartments were sold, and we had to move. It took a while to find somewhere to live, a decent playgroup and preschool.

'The lack of stability can't have helped,' our counsellors say.

'Even though we've been living where we are now for three years?' We hear the tension in our husbands' voices. They've had enough and don't want to come here anymore. Our husbands are convinced there's nothing wrong with our parenting. 'Daniel's never liked hanging around other kids—being touched even—not since he was born.'

'Are you sure it's been since birth?' Our counsellors are sceptical. It's their job to make us see sense.

'Absolutely sure,' we say.

'Well, maybe it's just the way he is then?' They make a note in their manila folder.

'But what kid doesn't like friends, hugs, or being told that he's loved?' we ask, though we already know the answer—our kid. Last night, we told Daniel/Michael/George that he was doing a good job of brushing his teeth. But he just shouted at us. *Don't say that, Mummy, don't say I'm doing well!* He simply doesn't respond the way other kids do. 'Surely there's something we can do?'

Our counsellors shake their heads. 'It sounds like you'll just have to live with it.'

Tears well again. We love cuddling our children, even when Daniel/Michael/George pushes us away. We'll never stop hoping that one day they'll cuddle us back.

The counsellors notice the tears in our eyes. 'Look, all you can really do for him is provide a stable environment, talk gently but act firm, reserve one-on-one time for him, and teach him about his emotions.' *All you can really do for him.* The words repeat through our minds, and we add, *until he's gone.*

He already looks like he's fading. He's so skinny. We feed him organic meat and vegetables; we cook everything fresh. Yet he won't put on weight.

Wiping our eyes, we notice Daniel/Michael/George sitting on the orange or grey or speckled carpet tiles of our counsellors' office, playing with a pirate ship. His eyes are intense, his concentration solid. He's trying to get at the pirate figures inside the ship. When he finds the latch on the ship's side, and its deck springs open, he smiles. Perhaps he's bored at home?

For the next month, our focus is entertainment. We take our kids out twice a day, every day. We take them swimming and to friends' houses. We go to playgrounds and indoor play centres. We do craft, read books and learn the alphabet. Still, when we try to help our children draw the letter 'G', they rip the paper away. When we try reading to them, they fidget, grabbing and trying to flip the pages.

'Hold on, Daniel, I haven't finished reading this page yet.'

'But I want to turn over.'

'Well, there's no point until I've read this page.'

'But—I—want—to!'

Sarah/Selina/Santi nuzzles against our other arm, yawning. She's not really listening to the story, just enjoying the snuggle.

'Fine,' we say to Daniel/Michael/George, remembering what our counsellors told us about having realistic expectations of our children. Perhaps he's too young for practising letters or reading? After all, he's still in nappies at night. Sometimes he not only soaks the nappy, he soaks the bed too.

Daniel/Michael/George smiles, takes the book, and turns each page until he reaches the end. Meanwhile we make a mental note to Google it all later—much later. We're yawning, so tired now. So when the kids go for their day nap, we take one too. For once, we leave the washing up and the laundry, and just pass out. When the sound of children squabbling wakes us, we try to call out but realise we can't. Throats sore, eyes throbbing, now we're getting sick.

Days later, we can't cope anymore. Our husbands took time off work when we first got sick, but now the kids are sick too. Throats still sore, and in need of antibiotics, we go to our doctors. At short notice we have to see different doctors than usual. After checking our throats and printing out the appropriate prescriptions, they check our children's throats too.

'Does he snore at all?' they ask after peering inside Daniel/Michael/George's mouth and nose.

'Like a train,' we tell him.

'And does he breathe through his mouth much?'

'All the time—eating, watching television, doing puzzles.'

'And has anyone mentioned sleep apnoea to you?' The doctors turn to look at us, the worried mothers that we are. 'His tonsils are the biggest I've ever seen.'

We shake our heads. 'What's sleep apnoea?'

'If it's alright with you, we'll take an x-ray of his adenoids.' The adenoids, they explain, are the lymph tissue behind the nose. 'Just in case. Does he hold his breath at night?'

'I don't know. Why, is it serious?'

'It can be.'

That afternoon, we go for x-rays. The results show Daniel/Michael/George's adenoids to be almost twice the normal size. The doctors refer us to specialists. When we get home, we rush to our computers and Google 'sleep apnoea'. It's a severe form of sleep-disordered breathing that can lead to death. After reading through the information, we phone our husbands.

'Listen to this,' we demand as soon as they answer. 'These are the symptoms for sleep apnoea: moodiness, irritability; hyperactivity, lack of attention; aggressive behaviour; snoring, mouth breathing; daytime tiredness; poor weight gain; bed-wetting; and…depression.'

'That's everything!' our husbands say, shocked.

'I know. And it says here that enlarged adenoids and tonsils can actually stop oxygen from reaching his brain at night. So…I know it's going to cost us, but we need to see this specialist.'

'Definitely. As soon as we can.'

'I've booked an appointment for Friday,' we say, wondering why no one else had ever suggested sleep apnoea.

That Friday, the specialists sigh when they examine Daniel/Michael/George. 'Doesn't eat anything chewy, am I right? No steak, no chops. Only mince I expect.'

We pause to think. We've always assumed our children's preference for mince was a kid thing.

'And he's been a bit trying to deal with lately, yes?'

We nod.

'Well, don't worry about that anymore. It's all going to change.'

'What do you mean?'

'I see this all the time. Adenoids have to come out of course, tonsils too. But in a few months you'll have an entirely different boy.'

We smile but don't really believe what the specialists tell us. If it were that easy, if they see this all the time, surely someone would have said something before now? The specialists have only one explanation when we ask them. 'Not everyone knows about it.'

We think about each other then, all those other mothers out there suffering, and we want to reach out. *It'll be okay,* we want to tell each other, *it's really going to be okay.*

That night, we watch with our husbands as our children sleep. They snore loudly, but occasionally fall silent. We lick our palms and hold them over Daniel/Michael/George's nose and mouth. There's no breath. We count to fifteen, then there's a massive intake of air and the snoring starts again. Our hearts sink when we realise our poor children haven't had decent sleep their entire lives. For them, it must be like 3 am all day, every day.

Six months later, adenoids and tonsils removed, Daniel/Michael/George runs to us across the school playground…for a hug.

'Had a good day, darling?'

'Yes, Mummy.'

'Good.' We relish the feel of him, squeezing us close. 'Here's your list.' We pass him the shopping list he drew this morning, with pictures of fruit and vegetables and the numbers we need alongside them. His best subject at school is math and, although he still hates singing and dancing, he can happily sit for hours now while we read to him.

'Yay! Thank you, Mummy, I love you so much!' He jumps in excitement.

'I love you too, darling.' We nod towards Sarah.

He rolls his eyes but says it anyway. 'Hello, Sarah.'

We've been at him a lot lately to be nicer to his sister. He's still reluctant, but he probably always will be. After all, he was here first.

At the supermarket, though, we see him trying.

'You hold the bag,' he tells her, 'I'll put the apples in.'

'I want to put them in too!' she says.

'Why don't you take turns?' we say, finally able to use that calm tone of voice we used to hear other mothers using.

Later, as we load our shopping into our car, we hear a car door slam, or a sob, and we look behind us. A woman is leaning against her car, her hands over her ears, rocking herself. Through the windows of her car, we notice two children, maybe three, screaming and pulling at each other.

'Are you okay?' we call out.

When she looks up, there are tears streaming down her face. We recognize her. She's one of us.

'Hold on!' We tell Daniel/Michael/George and Sarah/Selina/Santi to wait in the car, and we walk over to the woman. We have no idea if we can help, but we need to try. Our children's future is no longer the inevitable demise we once dreaded. Our fear of losing them, of losing either of our children, is just that—a fear, nothing more. In fact, the only thing we know now with absolute certainty is that we can't let another family suffer just because we didn't say something.

We smile at the woman and ask again if she's okay.

A HOUSE FOR THE WAZUNGU
Anne Goodwin

THE day the helicopter came, it hovered over our village like an airborne hippo, rocking the sky with the buzz of a churchful of bees. The children threw down their pencils and raced out to the football field to wave. We parents were not so readily impressed; we might have raised our heads from our work and squinted up against the sun, but only for as long as it took to wipe the sweat from our brows. We knew that no helicopter could help us get our maize planted or cook the ugali at the end of the day, so we continued working. All but Albert Lumumba. What could he do? A man cannot call himself a teacher unless he has pupils to teach.

By all accounts, he reached the football field in time to see the broad-shouldered men in dark glasses step down onto the rough grass, to watch them hand out sweets in cellophane wrappers to the children. Just in time to clap his hands and draw his pupils' attention to how the blades that lifted the machine into the sky were shaped like the wings of a bird, as if the sudden appearance of two men from the city were part of his lesson plan.

Albert Lumumba escorted the visitors back to the school. He invited them to sit on stools in the shade of the great thatched roof and watch his pupils perform their song and dance of welcome. He sent one of the children to Miriam Moto's stall to fetch chai in china cups. What else could he do? Visitors, however noisy and inconvenient, must be entertained.

Before the sun went down, Albert Lumumba called us to the school to meet the strangers from the city. He said they had a message that concerned us all. We sat cross-legged on the floor while the broad-shouldered men explained that if we built a brick house with its own latrine, wazungu would come and spread dollars around our village.

We laughed. Why would the wazungu want to come to Kanini? Wazungu like to see elephants, crocodiles and leopards. Elephants that trample the crops in the fields. Crocodiles that steal the best bathing places in the rivers. Leopards that snatch sleeping babies from their hammocks. Fortunately, or unfortunately, we have no elephants, crocodiles or leopards in Kanini. Only a few cows and a herd of goats.

The city men shook their heads. In their dark glasses we couldn't see their eyes. 'The wazungu are interested in more than our country's wildlife,' they said. 'They want to meet you. Watch you smooth cow-dung over the floors of your huts. Carry water home from the spring on your heads. Wash your clothes in the river and hang them over the bushes to dry in the sun. They want to learn how you live your lives.'

And then we knew that wearing dark glasses or living in the city or flying through the sky in a giant hippo, deafened by the drone of a churchful of bees, had made these men mad. For if there was one thing we all knew about the wazungu, it was that they never wanted to learn from us. They wanted to tell us to have fewer children. They wanted to take pictures of our too many children and display them in their homes. They wanted to harvest our seeds and sell them back to us at planting time. They wanted to preach and they wanted to steal, but they didn't want to learn.

But we couldn't send our visitors back to the city disappointed. We told them, 'Albert Lumumba is the best teacher Kanini has ever had. If it's learning the wazungu want, send them to him. Go ahead and build your brick house with its private latrine. Albert Lumumba will help them learn.'

Even before they arrived, even before their house was built, the wazungu found ways to preach at us. They insisted that clay bricks baked hard in the sun weren't solid enough for a wazungu house. Their house required factory bricks with sharp edges and words stencilled onto the top. They let us know that wazungu do not trouble themselves to squat to evacuate their bowels, but must sit comfortably on a latrine with a seat. Even the children, who had watched open-mouthed as the house took shape, laughed at this. Their parents noticed, and smiled, but only for as long as it took to wipe the sweat from our brows.

And so the time came for the flying hippo to deposit the first wazungu in Kanini. Albert Lumumba took them to the school where the children danced their welcome dance and sang their welcome song. The wazungu looked bewildered. They refused the chai from Miriam

Moto's stall, and we worried that they might not have brought any dollars to spread around. Then a lorry arrived and they began to smile. We gasped. The lorry contained nothing but water: a great tank for their baths; another to throw down their private latrine with a seat; yet more water in clear plastic bottles for them to drink. For the wazungu could not walk all the way to the spring, or drink from a glass with worms wriggling at the bottom.

Gradually, we got to know the routine. Every three days or so, the helicopter would drop down on the football field and four wazungu would step out to begin their education. They would sit in the sun for a few days until their skin turned pink, and then the helicopter would return and swap them for another four wazungu. At first, they didn't trouble us much. Neither did we ask ourselves whether they were learning. We fetched our water and weeded our crops and searched for firewood, just as we'd always done.

In time, the wazungu became bolder. Or more curious. They started to venture further into the village, beyond the triangle of football field, school and the factory-brick house. They handed out gifts: sweets for the children; beer for the men; clothes they'd grown tired of for the women. At first, we were pleased: the children no longer complained of hunger; the men no longer worried about the rains; the women once again felt like singing when we got dressed in the morning. But soon wives began to grumble; the men no longer worried about getting up from their blankets and going out to the fields. Walking along the pot-holed road to her chai stall, Miriam Moto fell off her glittery slingbacks and twisted her ankle. Albert Lumumba realised that his pupils preferred sweets to ugali and, although they were no longer hungry, their concentration on lessons had not improved.

The broad-shouldered men returned for another meeting. We would have been happy to see the wazungu house dismantled brick by factory brick, but Albert Lumumba urged us to give them another chance. He reminded us what wazungu dollars could give our children: roast chicken on Sundays; school desks and books, enough for every child; maybe, in time, a clinic in Kanini itself.

So we let the city men in their sunglasses tell us more about the wazungu. We learnt that, while they might all look alike, with their pointy noses and albino skin, the wazungu have different tribes, with different values and customs, just as we do. We'd heard of the Missionary who made our grandmothers cover their breasts. The vee-ess-oh who would arrive without a word of Kiswahili, but fluent in the language of a village two days' walk away. So we were prepared to accept that the problem might not be with wazungu as a whole, but with the particular tribe that had come to Kanini. The Tourists didn't suit our ways. When the rains came, they didn't whoop for joy, happy that the maize would grow or thankful their roof didn't leak. Instead, these Tourists grumbled about the noise on their corrugated-iron roof, and complained about getting soaked on the way back from the latrine.

The broad-shouldered men would bring us a different tribe. A wazungu tribe who really would want to learn. We looked forward to meeting the Travellers. But only for as long as it took to wipe the sweat from our brows.

At first, this new tribe seemed even less accommodating than the Tourists. They made their way to Kanini by jeep, denying us the spectacle of the helicopter dropping down from the sky. Instead of dressing up in their Sunday suits, as we would whenever we went visiting, their clothes were shabby and worn. When the children asked these wazungu for sweets they shook their heads, and offered to teach them a song. As if a song could fill their stomachs! And instead of sitting outside the wazungu house all day, they followed us out to the fields and into the forest, calling out *Jambo* and getting in our way.

We tried to ignore them, but they just smiled and grabbed an adze and copied us hacking at the hard earth. Or raised a bundle of sticks onto their shoulders and carried it back to our shacks. Or followed Albert Lumumba into the school and showed the children their tribal dance which they called the hokey-cokey.

The Travellers also bestowed gifts upon the village. But these weren't like the gifts the Tourists had brought. There was a radio that had a handle we could turn to make it talk. There were solar-powered lights for our children so they could do their homework after dark. There were clay stoves that didn't eat up so much wood. There was even a bicycle taxi for getting to the clinic in the next village. These weren't the kind of gifts that serve as a prelude to preaching or stealing. These were things we would have asked for ourselves, had we known they existed.

~ 183

In return, we showed them the rhythms of our lives. And so, in time, the wazungu became our friends. Some of them came back year after year, and their names became as familiar as those of our neighbours. There was Christine who was always ready to join in a dance, bracelets jangling as she clapped her hands, and her husband, Matthew, with his passion for cooking ugali, beating it hard in the pot so there were never any lumps. They came in the dry season and they came in the wet. Then, one year, they came with a baby.

We were shocked at our first sight of a white baby. Completely taken aback, as if we'd assumed wazungu arrived on earth fully grown, never having to suffer the indignity of learning. We were troubled by the pallor of his milky skin, afraid that with so flimsy a barrier against the hazards around him, he would not survive.

Yet survive he did, to return the next year. And the next. Halili. Beloved. Symbol of the bond between the Traveller tribe and the people of Kanini. We looked forward to watching him grow alongside our own children.

When it was time for the elections, the broad-shouldered men in dark glasses landed their helicopters in the football field to show us where we should mark our cross. The wazungu stayed away, but we weren't concerned. We assumed they were busy voting in their own countries.

Christine and Matthew and Halili were the first to return. We rushed to the wazungu house to dance the hokey-cokey. They went through the actions but behind their smiles we could see their eyes were sad. The little boy was fretful. Mothers scooped him up and squeezed him to our breasts but it took a long time to soothe him.

Matthew told Albert Lumumba about the roadblocks all the way from the airport: groups of young men angry at the results of our elections, saying some tribes had put their crosses in the wrong place.

Miriam Moto ushered Matthew to her compound. Begged him to cook his delicious ugali on her energy-efficient stove. Chanting girls formed a circle around Christine, nudging her into a celebratory dance. Infants collected up their makeshift toys to tempt Halili: a discarded water bottle half-full of pebbles, dolls made of dried fronds of palm. We wanted our friends to forget the trials of their journey. We wanted them to be happy in Kanini.

The day after Miriam Moto's field was set alight, burning the sorghum and maize that should have sustained her through the lean months, the helicopter came down in the football field once more. The broad-shouldered men, who had never seemed to raise a sweat before, raced to the wazungu house. Out came Christine and Matthew and little Halili and all their baggage. They hugged each of us in turn, while the men from the city urged them to hurry along. We followed them to the football field. No one was waving. No one was singing. No one was dancing the hokey-cokey.

As the helicopter blades began to spin, Christine seemed to hesitate. Tears streaking down her face, she pleaded with her rescuers for them to take us too. All of us. One of us. It made no difference. There was no room for the people of Kanini in the flying hippo.

After all the fields had been set alight and our crops destroyed, we needed a place to hide. We rushed to the wazungu house. With its brick walls, solid door and corrugated-iron roof, it would be more secure than our own huts. But the door was locked, and we didn't have the time to find the tools to hack through the padlock. So we ran to the church which, while made of wood and thatch, might at least have God's protection. And there was space for us all. We piled in, barricaded the door and began to pray.

When we heard the mob hissing outside, telling us our votes were wrong, that we had no right to our land, we remembered the Tourists who had come first to Kanini, their ears full of helicopter buzz. When we smelled the burning thatch, we thought of the Travellers, their nostrils filled with the fresh water that would wash away the stench of fear when they reached their homes. When we felt the smoke choking our throats, we asked ourselves what tribe would come next to Kanini. This was not a lesson the wazungu would welcome into their hearts.

Albert Lumumba's voice rose above the screams of his pupils. 'Journalists will come,' he said, 'to tell of this atrocity.'

Maybe, we thought. But who will be left to greet them; who will go to the wazungu house to dance our welcome dance and sing our welcome song?

For details on other available titles, and for information on individual contributors to this anthology, please visit the Chuffed Buff Books' website.

www.chuffedbuffbooks.com

CPSIA information can be obtained at www.ICGtesting.com
Printed in the USA
BVOW05s1711210815

414029BV00002B/19/P

9 781908 858023